"Now, this one is for you,"

Benedict said, dipping another strawberry in his wine.

He dangled it seductively under her nose. It looked luscious. Each time she started to bite it, he moved it ever so slightly toward his own mouth. She knew what he was doing. It was a sneaky way to steal a kiss.

"You've got this all backward," Stephanie said. "It was Eve who tempted Adam, not the other way around." Immediately she knew she shouldn't have said it.

"So it was. I'll gladly yield if you want to be the seducer, but I thought you were a little slow in getting started." He brushed the strawberry lightly across her lips. "Do you want to seduce me?"

"I'll give you a strawberry if you want one, but I don't do seductions."

"Maybe you'll change your mind."

Dear Reader,

Welcome to Silhouette—experience the magic of the wonderful world where two people fall in love. Meet heroines that will make you cheer for their happiness, and heroes (be they the boy next door or a handsome, mysterious stranger) who will win your heart. Silhouette Romance reflects the magic of love—sweeping you away with books that will make you laugh and cry, heartwarming, poignant stories that will move you time and time again.

In the coming months we're publishing romances by many of your all-time favorites, such as Diana Palmer, Brittany Young, Sondra Stanford and Annette Broadrick. Your response to these authors and our other Silhouette Romance authors has served as a touchstone for us, and we're pleased to bring you more books with Silhouette's distinctive medley of charm, wit and—above all—*romance*.

I hope you enjoy this book and the many stories to come. Experience the magic!

Sincerely,

Tara Hughes
Senior Editor
Silhouette Books

KERRIE GRAY

Love Is
a Gypsy

Silhouette *Romance*

Published by Silhouette Books New York

America's Publisher of Contemporary Romance

SILHOUETTE BOOKS
300 E. 42nd St., New York, N.Y. 10017

ISBN: 0-373-08666-0

First Silhouette Books printing August 1989

KERRIE GRAY,

a former school principal and teacher, lives with her husband in Vienna, Virginia. She has quite a love for music; she enjoys opera, sings in a church choir and plays in an English handbell choir. The author and her husband enjoy bicycling, swimming and hiking in the mountains.

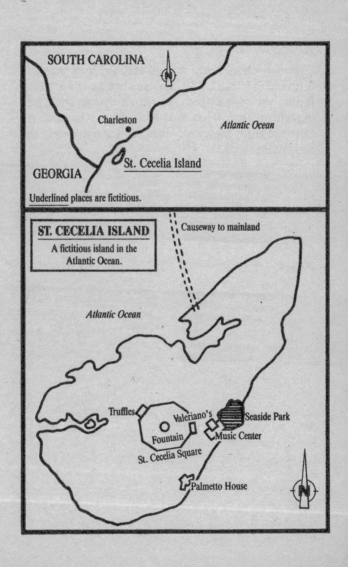

SOUTH CAROLINA

Charleston

Atlantic Ocean

St. Cecelia Island

GEORGIA

Underlined places are fictitious.

ST. CECELIA ISLAND

A fictitious island in the
Atlantic Ocean.

Causeway to mainland

Atlantic Ocean

Truffles

Valeriano's

Seaside Park

Fountain

Music Center

St. Cecelia Square

Palmetto House

N

Chapter One

Relax, relax," Stephanie Morrison fiercely reminded herself for at least the hundredth time that morning. But in spite of her good intentions, she fidgeted nervously in her chair and once again consulted the clock on the classroom wall. It was ten minutes to twelve. In exactly two hours and ten minutes everything she had learned about singing during her four years in college as a music major would be put to the test in an audition for the title role of *Carmen*. The opera was to be presented by the St. Cecelia Summer Opera Workshop at season's end in late August. To win that role would be a dream come true. Stephanie had never wanted anything so much in all her twenty-two years, and musically she felt she was ready for it.

Overachiever that she was, she had practiced hours and hours preparing the aria she would sing this afternoon for the audition. If only she could sing it as well today as she had yesterday! If only she could stop these jitters so her musicianship could shine through her singing! She closed her eyes and drew a deep breath, chanting silently to herself, "Breathe in peace, breathe out tension." Several times she repeated the calming ritual, only to have her tremors return the minute she opened her eyes.

Nine minutes to twelve. Stephanie came back to the business at hand, lost at the tail end of a workshop on how to sing smoothly connected passages in German. She wished the class was over. Obviously the instructor was bent on keeping them until the very stroke of twelve.

With an excess of energy, she thrust her notebook and pen into her tote bag and—wouldn't you know it?—knocked over her umbrella. It landed with a clattering smack, barely missing the foot of the red-haired Dierdre, who sat next to her. Stephanie offered an embarrassed smile and mouthed "Sorry" when her neighbor looked around at the sudden noise. After retrieving the umbrella and hooking it over her arm, she waited out the last five minutes of the workshop hunched over a stomachful of butterflies that had been gathering all morning in spite of her attempts to stay calm.

The moment of liberation finally came, and Stephanie, carefully dodging the dawdlers and talkers, hurried down the corridor toward the lobby of the Music Center to meet Lynne Kendrick, her roommate, and Nicholas Bartoni, their new tenor friend, for lunch at Valeriano's.

In the glass-enclosed lobby a traffic jam of shorts, sundresses and faded jeans was forming between the potted fig trees that framed the entrance. The crowd spilled out onto the terrace, but stood in little knots pressed up against the glass under the shelter of the roof overhang. Stephanie, standing apart and searching the group for her friends, was dismayed at the sudden blossoming of umbrellas outside. Rain!

Just then Lynne and Nick arrived, surveyed the situation and came up with a similar conclusion, which they announced simultaneously.

"But I'm well prepared," said Nick, brandishing his big black umbrella. "Oh, you have one, too, Stephanie. That's great. Let's get out of here before this mob does or we'll never get a table."

"You two go ahead," urged Stephanie, "I don't want to get my shoes wet."

Nick frowned in perplexity. "Why would you wear those shoes on a day when you need an umbrella?"

"It won't make much sense, but I'll tell you anyway. For good luck, that's why."

"You don't need good luck," said Nick. "I've heard you sing."

"Besides," said Stephanie, "the weather service said there was only a thirty percent chance of rain, so I wore them, hoping that it wouldn't. But I brought my umbrella just in case it did."

"Why didn't you bring some old shoes also? Lots of women carry walking shoes in their bags." Nick, it seemed, just wasn't going to let it alone.

"Oh, I don't know," she said, beginning to feel a little foolish. "I should have. I just didn't think of it, I guess. Why don't you and Lynne go on over and save a table? If it hasn't stopped in a few minutes, I'll take off my shoes and come padding over in my little stocking feet."

She watched the crowd part and then close around Nick and Lynne as they went out the door. The big black umbrella opened, and the two, huddled under it, stepped out into the rain. He, built like a teddy bear—and just as lovable—seemed impervious to the weather. Lynne, slender and blond, clung to his arm and tiptoed gingerly, dodging puddles and splashes.

Maybe she had been unrealistic in dressing this morning, but the idea of wearing this particular ensemble on this particular day had been so pleasing she just couldn't let go of any part of it. The red shoes matched her dress, a gift from her mother, who was trying to wean her from a wardrobe of faded, worn-out jeans. She loved the dress with its free-form red geraniums on a white background. It had big, round, puffy sleeves, a scoop neckline that was outrageously flattering, and a full, flirty skirt. The gleam of pearls in her necklace and in her earrings made her feel polished and well put together. The umbrella, though, added the special touch—an exhilarating sense of destiny. It, too, was red, and along one of its ribs, white block letters spelled out her dream—the Metropolitan Opera.

After a moment Stephanie decided to go outside for a better look at the sky. Black clouds, looking heavy enough for a thunderstorm, were piling up fast. A wind had come up, and in spite of the overhang, the rain blew in on her. She unfurled her umbrella.

She'd better go. Already it was raining harder. Wishing now that she had yielded to plain common sense about today's costume, she set down her tote bag and bent over, under the shield of her umbrella, to unbutton the straps of her shoes.

Suddenly she was startled by the appearance of a pair of well-polished brown loafers with little fringed tassels that stepped up beside her. Where had they come from? She had been so preoccupied she hadn't even heard their approach. Twin columns of khaki twill rose above them. She straightened up past a blue oxford-cloth shirt and a tanned hairy arm. The view was crowned by a classical profile and a neat cap of dark curly hair. When she was totally upright, the head ducked, and suddenly hairy arm, blue shirt and khaki twill were all under the umbrella close to her.

"Hello," he said in a rich, resonant baritone with a smile in it.

"Hey! Wait a minute!" she said, a warning note in her voice. "Not so fast. What do you think you're doing?" She raised the umbrella far above their heads, backed away from him, then pulled it down close to her own head, making it perfectly obvious, she thought, that her umbrella was not a public shelter.

"Sorry I startled you. I thought you had seen me coming."

"Seen you? I saw your feet when you were a mere three inches away. I don't mean to be rude," she continued, "but it is a little disconcerting to have someone sprout up so fast and so close with no warning, especially when you don't know what he's up to."

"Again, I'm sorry. I really didn't mean to frighten you. I haven't the slightest intention of picking your pocket or anything like that, if that's what you're afraid of." His smile was almost disarming.

"Well, what *were* your intentions?" Then she remembered Lynne and Nick waiting for her, and glanced at her watch. "If you can be brief. I've got to go in two minutes."

"Brief it shall be. Actually all I intended was to ask you for directions to Truffles. The restaurant? Could you point me in the right direction? I drove in from Charleston after dark last night, and I don't know where anything is except the rental car agency."

His request was so reasonable and his voice so earnest that she began to soften toward him. "Yes," she replied, willing now to be pleasant and helpful. "This walk will take you straight into St. Cecelia Square," she said, pointing to the left. "You can see it from here."

As he bent to look around the umbrella in the direction she indicated, she caught just a drift of a woodsy fragrance, subtle and pleasing. She hadn't noticed it earlier. "Truffles is on the other side of the square. You can't see the restaurant from here because that statue is in the way, but it has gray shutters and a gray fringed awning, and it's right beside the Bank of South Carolina."

"That sounds easy enough. Thanks," he said.

"You can't miss it. When you get to the square, you'll find a covered walk all the way around, so at least for part of the way you'll be out of the rain."

"That's great," he said, looking down at the rain splashing and puddling on the pavement. "But I'll be drenched before I get halfway there."

"Why don't you wait a few minutes until it slackens?"

"I can't. I've got an appointment at noon with some newspaper guy."

Stephanie looked at her watch. "You're late. It's ten after already. I'm late, too. I've just got to go."

"Which direction are you going? If you don't mind my asking."

"That way." She pointed to the square again.

His brown eyes lit up. "To the square?"

"Yes, to Valeriano's. I'm meeting friends for lunch. They're probably wondering where I am."

"Would you mind if I walked with you that far? That reporter guy is probably gnashing his teeth wondering where I am."

Stephanie didn't respond but merely looked at him, frowning a little.

"I'm perfectly harmless," he continued. "I won't attack you. I promise." He gave her another smile, half appeal, half mischief, but oddly charming.

"Oh, that's not it. I trust you."

"Good, let's go then." Reaching for the umbrella, he asked, "Why don't you let me take that?" Then he offered her the crook of his arm. "And you take this."

She backed away. He advanced, saying, "Don't be shy," and linked his arm through hers.

Then Stephanie felt the most unexpected thing—a sudden and acute sensation of arm against arm. His burned hers, and she experienced a strange craving for warmth. Right in the middle of wondering if he, too, was experiencing the same thing, she realized that not a butterfly was fluttering a wing in her stomach. They were gone. She was free of the jitters. Relief washed over her like a blessing. She had, until that moment, totally misunderstood the true purpose of umbrellas.

"Ready? Let's go." His arm was compelling, and she almost followed it until she suddenly remembered her shoes.

"Not now. It's raining too hard. We'll get drenched. Maybe it'll slacken in a minute." She would not be moved.

"Slacken? Look at the sky. It's getting worse by the minute. We'd better go while we can. Besides, isn't this what umbrellas are for? Hang on, let's go." He continued trying to urge her off the step, but she, uncoupling, retreated.

From her position somewhat behind him how, she said, "It isn't the umbrella. It's my shoes. They're new. I don't want to get them wet."

"Oh, I see," he said.

"You don't understand," she accused him. "I paid a pile of money for these shoes. Too much. I don't want to ruin them."

Glancing up at the sky, then back to her, he said, "I know it's none of my business, but I was just wondering why you would wear such shoes on a day like this."

She had heard that question before, but she said simply, "I wanted to look nice. It's very important that I look nice today."

"You do. You look very nice, indeed, and that's a nice dress. Pretty color. That's about the color of crape myrtles, isn't it?"

"No, I don't think so. This is just a plain, old, everyday geranium red."

"Well," he said after a moment, holding the umbrella out to her, "I'm late and getting later. I'd better go. Take care of your shoes." Since she didn't take the umbrella, he set it down beside her and turned to go.

A little touch of charity pricked at her heart. "Wait," she said. "You're going to get sopping wet. I'll take off my shoes and put them in my bag. Then we can go. Just a second."

One shoe was off and in the bag when he said, "Put it back on. I've a better idea. Here, you take the umbrella."

Before she realized what he intended, he, without a word of warning other than an "upsy-daisy," scooped her up and tossed her across his shoulder. He clamped his arms around her knees to hold her in place and strode off into the storm.

"Sorry I can't call up a carriage with four white horses," he called to her. "This is the best I can do, but at least it will save your shoes."

"No! No! This is crazy. Put me down, put me down."

"You'll get your shoes wet if I do. Hold the umbrella over this way. I'm getting wet."

"Sorry. My arms don't work that way. Let's go back," she yelled. "This is not very comfortable. Go back. Please. Your shoulder is hurting my stomach."

"I can't hear a word you're saying back there," he complained, shouting. "If you want me to hear you, you'll have to speak up. Look, I'm getting drenched. Can't you hold that umbrella more to the left?"

Her rear end was up where her head should have been, and any attempt to "speak up" would be directed straight to the small of his back. Bobbing along upside down in such an awkward position, she couldn't possibly raise her head to be heard and shelter them both with the umbrella. Besides, she had an appointment herself—not with just any newspaper guy, but with Benedict Delman, who just happened to be the most important person in the world to her today. She wanted to look professional for the audition, but how could she in a dress that had been soaked by the rain and crushed into a mass of wrinkles against this stranger's body?

An exasperated voice broke into her thoughts. "Would you let me have that umbrella? You're not holding it over me at all. Maybe I can hold it better than you."

"No way," she shouted back.

Just at that moment the moderate rain turned into a downpour—opaque, fierce, pounding. It dimpled the flood that deepened on the sidewalk and swirled and eddied in the gutters. In the small park they were passing, the onslaught beat the pink petunias flat, and sharp gusts set the pine trees to writhing as if in agony. Stephanie screamed as the wind smacked the sheet-like rain against them from all sides. Her once carefully curled hair, now

as wet as seaweed, was plastered across her face. Another violent gust thwacked them, whipping her full skirt
over her head and turning her brand new umbrella inside out. At the same instant she felt him stagger, buf-
feted by the blast. She screamed again and grabbed for
her skirt, and in that instinctive impulse to preserve
modesty, dropped her tote bag into the swirling waters.

"Stop! Stop! My bag! I've dropped my bag!" she
shouted almost in a frenzy.

He stopped and shouted a string of words that she
thought exactly suited the situation.

"No, don't put me down now. No, I said. I'll ruin my
shoes. You'll have to get it," she yelled, bending her
knees to keep her shoes high and dry.

"Well, I certainly can't get it with five hundred pounds
of screaming madwoman on my back."

He jerked off her shoes without unbuttoning them,
handed them around to her, and then stood her down on
the flooded sidewalk.

"You get it," he ordered, wiping the rain off his face.

"Ruined," she shouted, looking at the dark, wet circles mottling the fine leather of her shoes. "And it's all
your fault." She thrust them back at him to hold. "Ruined," she repeated, doing the same with the now-useless
umbrella. She sent him a red-hot glare.

Bunching her full skirt between her knees, she squat-
ted on her heels and began fishing for the scattered contents of her tote in the water and throwing them all,
dripping wet, back into her bag. When she straightened
up, she was angry and breathing hard. Her sopping dress
clung coldly to her back. Reclaiming her shoes, she saw
that he had been holding them right side up. They had
begun to fill with rain.

"Oh, look what you're doing! How could you be so stupid?" She grabbed the shoes and poured the water out. "They are totally ruined," she wailed, putting them into her bag. "It just absolutely kills me to have paid so much money for them and then have them ruined the first time I wear them."

"Now wait a minute," he said. "Aren't you overstating this? They're not ruined, they're just a little wet. They'll dry and be as good as new. However, I am sorry you got them wet."

"*I* got them wet! I suppose you had nothing to do with it," she screamed.

"I said I was sorry." He looked at her for a chilling moment, then flung her ruined umbrella at her feet and strode off without another word. She stood motionless, watching him break into a sprint. The rain pelted her head, flooded her eyes and poured off the end of her nose.

After retrieving her umbrella, she splashed down the street in her stocking feet, running as fast as she could until a stitch in her side made her slow down. When she reached her room on the second floor of Palmetto House, she jammed the twisted umbrella into a wastebasket and hurried into the bathroom. Unmindful of her sodden clothes and the water still streaming down her neck, she removed her shoes from the bag and carefully blotted them with a towel, then set them on the counter to dry. Tears smarted in her eyes. I will not cry, she thought fiercely. I will not. I won't be able to sing if I do.

Worrying that Lynne and Nick might delay placing their orders until her arrival, she hastily stripped. After quick work with a towel, she jumped into her old denim skirt and a pink polo shirt, as indifferent a costume as one could devise. In despair she combed her dripping hair. It hung dark and straight as a string to her shoulders, not a trace of her morning's curls left. She had dressed so carefully and now just look at her.

She considered leaving her wet clothes in a heap in the bathtub to be tended to later—but only for a second. Perfectionist that she was, she had to hang them up in a neat row on the shower rod before leaving. What a forlorn, droopy thing her dress was now! Its puffed sleeves had collapsed; its flattering scooped neckline sagged on the hanger.

She grabbed her wet tote bag, pounded down the steps, and ran through a light sprinkle to Valeriano's where Lynne and Nick listened in sympathy to an explanation about how the wind had turned her umbrella inside out, and the driving rain had drenched her and ruined her shoes after all. Missing from her story was the stranger who was probably sitting in Truffles this minute, soaking wet and freezing to death.

After a very light lunch of vichyssoise and iced tea—she didn't want to eat heavily just before singing and, besides, her jitters had returned—she ran back to her room wondering if she should waste precious time curling her hair and ironing her dress. She wanted to look nice, but she also needed every one of the forty-five minutes left before the audition to relax, first of all, and then to do a careful warm-up.

She looked at herself in the mirror—not much there to boost her self-confidence. If only her hair weren't so straight. A ponytail would have to do. Glancing at her watch again, she decided to simply make the most of what she had on by tying a scarf at her waist. A touch of mascara, a blush of pink clover and a slick of raspberry lip gloss, and she was ready. If she won the role of Carmen, it would be on merit alone. Why should it matter how she looked? But, in truth, it did matter. It mattered a great deal to her.

Just before leaving her room to go to the practice studio for the warm-up and final run-through, she scratched off a short good-luck note to Lynne, who was also auditioning for the role of Carmen.

On her way to the studio, she tried to get herself in the mood for her audition. She planned to sing the "Habañera," an aria from Act One of *Carmen*, which she loved for its sinuous, flamenco rhythms. As she walked along she imagined the gypsy girl Carmen, a cigarette factory worker, with unruly dark hair, flirting with the young men who keep asking when Carmen is going to love them. Carmen, looking straight at Don José, sings that love is a wild bird no one can tame, that love is a child of the gypsies who knows nothing of the law. Stephanie loved the way the music allows the voice to caress and warm the word *amour*, repeated over and over as Carmen tries to attract José's attention. When she finishes her song, Carmen flings a flower at his feet and runs away.

Upon reaching the studio and settling herself at the piano, Stephanie closed her eyes and repeated to herself, "I am perfectly calm and in complete control." Except, she thought, in my neck and shoulders, which are stiff with tension and in my heart, which is pounding violently. Then she opened her eyes and made a few desultory explorations up and down the scale, but it was weary work. Sighing, she stared at the keys for a while and tried again. She forced herself to plod through the "Habañera," then left for her appointment.

When she arrived at Rehearsal Hall B, she leaned against the wall and drew some slow, deep breaths. In a moment she knocked on the door, not because she was finally calm and relaxed, but because her watch said it was exactly two o'clock. Upon being invited to enter, she opened the door. Before her stood the stranger who had ruined her shoes. Now he seemed ten feet tall.

Both panic and despair seized her at once. Her first impulse was to back right out the door and run as fast as her legs would carry her, but she remained rooted to the spot.

"Come on in and close the door." His voice brought to a focus the business at hand. In response to his invitation, she did manage to close the door, but she didn't venture very far into the room. Stationing herself just in front of the door, she glanced about. Seated at the piano, the accompanist peered at her from behind wire-rimmed glasses and a sandy beard. Nearby, in one of the tan metal folding chairs, a man in jeans, an ankle propped on his knee, bent over a yellow pad busily writing. He looked briefly at her and went back to his work. She had seen them both around, but couldn't remember their names.

"I'm Benedict Delman," the stranger announced, striding all the way over to the door, his arm outstretched for a handshake, just as if she hadn't ridden his back a mere two hours ago. "I don't think we've met."

"Not actually."

"You must be Stephanie Morrison."

"Yes."

At first she had thought that perhaps he had not recognized her, so altered was her appearance; and she kept watching him for clues. Even after the introduction, she didn't know whether he did or not.

"Now, let me introduce Dave Hart, who will accompany you at the piano, and Phillip Downing, who is our stage director." As he indicated each with a wave of his hand, she nodded slightly. So far, so good, she thought, tightening her body against the tremors, hoping that she looked totally different from the girl in the rain. The problem was that she recognized him.

"Now, what role are you interested in?" His question made her knees weak.

"Carmen," she replied in a voice she hadn't heard since she was thirteen. She leaned back against the door, fighting for control of herself. She would not be intimidated. While he wrote something down in the notebook he was holding, she did a quick "breathe in, breathe out."

"What are you going to sing?" he asked.

"Habañera."

"Very good. Well, then, why don't you give Dave there the music, and we'll get under way."

Somehow she made it to the piano and turned to face the length of the room. Benedict and Philip went toward the back and sat down together. For several minutes there was silence. Then, finally, Dave at the piano said, "I'm ready when you are."

Humiliated, she murmured, "I'm sorry. I'm ready." She had forgotten her signal to the accompanist. The piano then began, but Stephanie's mind went blank. The music sounded strange. She struggled to grasp some familiar phrase that would help her get her bearings. She felt as if she had never heard any of it before. How could that be when she had practiced it for hours and hours? Yesterday she had sung it from memory. Panic again seized her. She looked at the door. It seemed to beckon. She must get hold of herself.

"I missed my entrance. Could we start over again, please?" Her throat felt tight; her heart hammered in her chest.

"Certainly. I'll bring you in," said Benedict.

"Oh, no. That's all right. I can do it."

When the piano started again, Benedict, disregarding her refusal of his help, stood and began conducting in small, indefinite movements. When it was time for her, he gave a big down beat with his right hand, while pointing to her with his left. She forced herself to concentrate, but she couldn't make her voice do one thing she wanted it to do. Nothing came out right. She wanted to show him all the shimmering, golden beauties of her voice; what she produced for him were thin, quavery little bleats. All through the ordeal Benedict watched her with an impassive face. When it was finally over, he came forward, insisted upon another handshake and said, "Thank you for coming by. We'll post the results Sunday morning after breakfast."

She nodded without saying anything and turned to leave.

"Stephanie, don't forget your music," called Dave, getting up from the piano to bring it to her. She thought she saw pity in his eyes.

Safely outside in the corridor, she slumped against the wall, her knees so weak she could barely stand. Closing her eyes, she let despair wash over her until she heard footsteps coming her way. Not wanting to be seen, she ran down the hall in the opposite direction and out the doors onto the beach where the sand was still wet and firm. Although the rain had stopped earlier, the sky had not cleared, and the beach looked gloomy and forlorn.

At her feet, an olive-green sea monotonously dashed against the gray shore. Angry and humiliated, Stephanie stood watching the great murky waves rising, curling, and fizzling out endlessly—such grand beginnings to such empty endings.

Then her eyes smarted and the whole scene turned blurry. Blinking furiously, she started walking along the deserted strand, past the gray weathered houses to where there was nothing but dunes, seagrass and occasional clumps of myrtle distorted by the wind. In the distance a dirty gray mist, thick and opaque, had obliterated landmarks. Sea and sky were blended in a pewter-colored vapor as if all creation had returned to its original chaos.

Too upset to think, Stephanie simply walked until she was so tired she could scarcely drag her feet over the wet sand. Eventually she walked back to the village, heading for the Bon Appetit Sandwich Shoppe. Perhaps a snack would make her feel better. Without much enthusiasm, she ordered a tuna sandwich and a glass of iced tea. To eat this late in the afternoon would ruin her appetite for dinner, but on this day of rampant ruination, one more thing wouldn't matter.

In the seclusion of her booth she slowly sipped a second glass of tea, making it last as long as possible, postponing minute by minute her return to the world of the opera workshop. She was sure failure was written all over her face and just as sure that triumph would be written on Lynne's. She dreaded the inevitable encounter; she was not at all sure she could take it in stride. Wasn't it strange, she mused, that nothing in her training had prepared her for failure? She had no idea of how to cope with it. She had always considered herself a winner.

A third glass of tea was out of the question; she would have to leave. Her bill paid, the tip calculated and carefully stacked by the edge of her plate, Stephanie rose to go, not feeling well. She shouldn't have eaten the sandwich; it had made her stomach queasy.

"Thank you. Have a nice afternoon," caroled the waitress.

"You have a nice afternoon, too," she responded.

Suddenly the telltale zig-zag of yellow light that always signaled the onset of a migraine flashed in her right eye. Oh, dear heavens, please, not that on top of everything else! That would be the absolute last straw. All at once, the most important thing in the world was to return to her room right this minute, whether Lynne was there or not. Fighting her nausea, she started for the door.

"Stephanie," a male voice called from nearby. She recognized it in an instant, and her heart sank. Annoyed, she glanced quickly in the direction from which it had come, and saw Benedict Delman in a booth between her and the door. A half-eaten hamburger and a cup of coffee were on the table in front of him.

"Stephanie," he called again, rising to come toward her. "May I have a word with you?"

The last thing she wanted right now was a word. She was desperate to get out of there. Her head spun, and she closed her eyes for a moment, then said, "Excuse me. I don't feel well."

"Do you need help?" he asked.

"No, I just need to go to my room as quickly as possible."

"I'll go with you."

"No, no, please," she said and stumbled past him and out the door.

Somehow, without remembering much about the short walk to Palmetto House, she reached her room, took an aspirin and closed the curtains. The darkened room was a bit much to insist upon with a roommate, but she would keep it that way, at least until Lynne returned. She lay down.

In half an hour or so, she heard Lynne's key in the lock. The door opened and then closed softly. For a second or two she listened to her roommate's careful, quiet sounds.

"I'm not asleep," she announced in a subdued voice.

"Are you okay? Anything I can do?"

Just then the telephone rang and Lynne picked up the receiver. Benedict Delman wanted to speak to Stephanie.

"No," she whispered fiercely.

A puzzled Lynne conveyed a softened answer. "Benedict, I'm sorry Stephanie can't come to the phone right now. May I take a message for her? Okay, no message. You didn't bother us at all. Bye, bye."

"Why won't you talk to Benedict?" Lynne asked after replacing the receiver.

"My head hurts terribly. Besides, I'm not ready."

"Not ready? What do you mean?" Lynne wanted to know.

"Do you have a minute? I had a bad experience today." Then in a flat, quiet voice, Stephanie told her story.

When she had finished, Lynne said, "That is just dreadful. I'd be upset, too. I think you should ask for another audition. It isn't fair for you to be judged under such circumstances."

"It wouldn't do any good. I don't think I could sing for him now, even if I wanted to."

Later, Lynne went down to dinner alone, leaving Stephanie to the welcome quiet of a darkened room. Lynne had been so eager to help that Stephanie had had a difficult time convincing her that there was no use in bringing up a dinner tray. She didn't feel like eating a bite.

After dinner Lynne returned and, standing in front of her closet, she tried to decide what to wear to the evening's recital. The musical season on St. Cecelia Island was in full swing now, with recitals, concerts, or ballets in the Music Center almost every night of the week. The members of the Opera Company could go for half price. All week, Stephanie had been looking forward to this recital, but now it seemed inconsequential.

After Lynne left, Stephanie replayed bits and pieces of the day's events in her mind. She thought of her ruined shoes. If she hadn't bought them in the first place, most likely she wouldn't be lying here with humiliation and failure as her bedfellows. What got into her, anyway, to make her think that she just couldn't live without them?

Those shoes had cost her a lot—eighty-four dollars, her self-confidence, plus the dream in her heart: the role of Carmen.

After a while she felt drowsy; her eyes, heavy. Red shoes for a Black Friday, she thought, and dropped off to sleep.

Chapter Two

The next morning, a Saturday, Stephanie opened her eyes to the dim light of the curtained window and squinted at the clock. It was nine. Lynne had left for her morning workshops so quietly that Stephanie hadn't even heard her. Stephanie drifted back into a restless sleep. Lynne returned to look in on her at midmorning break and again after lunch.

"I have something for you," she said. "Open your eyes."

"What is it?" Stephanie was groggy and not much interested, whatever it was.

"Just take a peek," Lynne insisted.

Obediently Stephanie made the effort, opening her eyes a mere slit. "Flowers? Oh, they're white daisies." There were only eight or ten of them, droopy things bundled with a blue rubber band. It was the sort of bouquet one might buy from a street vendor who was a little bit down on his luck, but Stephanie was touched. "Lynne, how sweet of you. Thanks so much. I guess we'll have to put them in a can."

"I'll do that but they're not from me," she said, beginning to strip the leaves off the bottom of the stems. "They're from Benedict."

"Isn't that odd? He hardly knows me. Why would he send me flowers? It makes me feel a little funny. I mean, I don't know quite what to think."

Lynne went into the bathroom, filled the can with water, and returned to set the artless bouquet on Stephanie's bedside table.

"Maybe it's his way of saying he's sorry about yesterday, or maybe it's just to say 'get well soon.' Whatever, I think he means well."

"I'll have to thank him," said Stephanie, as if it were a peculiar project not usually undertaken by ordinary people.

"Oh, before I forget," said Lynne, "there's something else. He gave me a note for you last night at the recital. Now, where did I put it? I thought I had it here in my purse." But she didn't find it, even after going through everything twice. Lynne was always misplacing things. "Oh, I know. It's probably in the pocket of that white skirt I wore last night. I'll get it now and put it right here beside your flowers. Sorry I didn't get it to you sooner, but you were asleep; and I forgot it this morning." She laid the note down on the table and then picked it back up. "Uh-oh. It says 'urgent' on it. Well, I hope it's not too urgent, if such a thing can be possible."

"Don't worry about it," Stephanie said.

Lynne started for the bathroom, but stopped and turned around to look at her roommate. "One more thing. Dierdre told me this morning that she didn't do very well at her audition yesterday, either, and she has scheduled another one for this afternoon. I wish you would consider it, Stephanie. I think you would feel better about yourself and him, too, if you did. Think about it.''

When Lynne went into the bathroom to brush her teeth, Stephanie picked up the note from Benedict. Why was it urgent? She squinted at her name scrawled on the envelope, and immediately the letters blurred and ran together. Her eyes ached terribly. She laid the note, unopened, back on the table and closed her eyes. ''Urgent'' wasn't strong enough a word to tempt her to read it now. As for another audition, the very thought of it brought back in full force all of yesterday's unconquered butterflies.

Stephanie heard Lynne come back into the bedroom. She opened her eyes and saw Lynne pick up a newspaper from her bed.

''You might be interested to know that the big news this morning was Benedict's interview,'' said Lynne. ''It's in today's paper. I went by the newsstand and bought one. I can't wait to see what it says.'' She reached for the switch of her reading lamp, then perched on the edge of her bed with the newspaper spread out beside her. Soon she was engrossed in the article. Stephanie, curious herself but reluctant to interrupt her, lay in silence watching her read.

''This is really interesting,'' commented Lynne, looking up briefly. ''I know he's not your favorite person right now, so I won't inflict this on you.''

''Oh, that's all right,'' said Stephanie, as close as she could come to admitting her curiosity. She had set him up as her nemesis, and she couldn't capitulate too soon without losing face.

''You might find just this tidbit interesting. Okay?''

"Okay."

"It says here that Benedict arrived for his interview late and soaking wet because of the sudden downpour."

"And because he got mixed up with this woman in red shoes," Stephanie added.

"No, it doesn't say a word about that. Too bad. After all that trouble, you didn't even make it into the newspapers." Lynne looked at her and smiled. "The reporter couldn't help saying that Benedict was a little brusque at first, but as the interview proceeded, he warmed up and became more pleasant and generous with his comments."

"Humph!" This from Stephanie to mask her interest.

"Want to hear any more?"

"It doesn't matter. I'll listen if you run across anything really juicy."

"How old would you guess him to be?" asked Lynne.

"I don't know. I can't guess men's ages. I can't guess much of anything about men," replied Stephanie.

"He's twenty-eight. It says here that he is considered by many to be one of the most promising young conductors in America. Aren't we lucky to have him here with us for the summer? Just think, when he's world famous, we can say we knew him when."

"I suppose it's luckier for some than for others. I, for one, don't feel very lucky," said Stephanie.

"I hope your luck changes before the summer's over," said Lynne, turning back to the paper. After a moment she had another morsel to share. "The reporter says Benedict was a sensation in Charleston this week, that he got rave reviews."

"What was he doing in Charleston?" Stephanie wanted to know.

"Well, he was supposed to be here for the beginning of our workshops, but at the last minute Emil Monteaux, the scheduled conductor for the symphony orchestra in Charleston, was taken to the hospital with chest pains, so they called Benedict and asked him to pinch-hit at the podium. That's why he didn't get here until Thursday night."

"No wonder he didn't know where Truffles was," mused Stephanie.

Then after quickly flipping past two or three pages and hunting down a column for the continuation of the article, Lynne said, "Here's something. It's not very juicy but it's interesting. He's going to make his debut as an opera conductor in our production of *Carmen*. He's really excited about it and says he has high hopes because he'll be working with such talented people. He calls us the 'cream of the crop,' some of the 'brightest and most promising young musicians this country has to offer.' That's us, Stephanie, so cheer up." Lynne shot her roommate a smile and continued. "Did you know this? We were chosen from a field of over six hundred applicants. Over a thousand young musicians tried out for the orchestra."

Stephanie was finding it all terribly interesting. "What else does it say?"

"Oh, the rest of it's mostly biographical. I won't upset you with it, but he talks about his childhood and his hobbies and let's see, oh, his career and about marriage."

"Oh," said Stephanie, her voice rising a little. "Is he married?"

"I don't know; I haven't read that part very carefully. I was just sort of scanning." Then she looked at the clock and suddenly jumped to her feet. "Look what time it is.

I hate to run, Stephanie, but I've got a tennis date with Hal Piersen in about ten minutes."

"Is he that tall, slender blonde?" asked Stephanie.

"Yes. Isn't he handsome? I think he looks like a Viking. He's really nice. He's in my workshop on acting for the singer. Every day he asks me to play tennis with him, and every day I say it's too hot. I'm just not accustomed to this South Carolina heat and humidity. I finally decided I might as well do it and get it over with. I'll probably die of sunstroke." She folded the newspaper and placed it on the bed beside her purse. "Since Benedict is not exactly your man of the hour, I'm going to take this article for Hal to read." Within minutes she had changed into her tennis togs and was out the door.

Left alone, Stephanie rose from her bed, opened the curtains and looked out upon a blazing blue and beige world of sand, sea and sky. Parades of bikinis and bare chests streamed by. A sand castle, which would be gone by morning, was under construction by a sand-pail crew. Beyond them a gentle surf splashed just enough to make the children squeal with delight and then run like sandpipers when the waves curled and collapsed. Not a cloud was in sight, and the sunlight shimmered above the water, touching its surface with a golden sheen.

Stephanie felt a surge of happiness, and all at once her room seemed too small and too dull. What was she going to do with herself all afternoon? She could go to the practice studio and work on her music, but she would probably end up almost cross-eyed after staring at little black notes until dinnertime. Then she made a decision to do what had been in the back of her mind ever since Lynne had left with the article about Benedict. She was going out to buy a newspaper, an errand she would not disclose to her roommate, who had folded shut her own paper right in the middle of the very best part.

After a shower, she crawled into some shorts and a cool, cotton shirt. Shielded from the sun by a floppy straw hat and dark glasses, she set out for the square. Although the sun was hot, a breeze from the ocean rattled the leathery fronds of the palms that lined the walk around St. Cecelia Square. At the newsstand the clerk said, "Sorry, miss. Sold out by ten o'clock this morning. Had a run on them. Try the drugstore and the supermarket."

To follow his suggestion meant a four-block hike down St. Cecelia Boulevard, for neither store was included in the ring of exclusive shops and boutiques that surrounded the square. She was lucky at the drugstore. On the spot she carefully tore out the interview, folded it, and stashed it away in her tote bag. Tomorrow she would read it. The rest of the paper she deposited in a container that admonished her to help keep St. Cecelia clean. Satisfied with her mission, she returned to the square, went into Truffles, the scene of the interview, just to see what it was like, and ordered an iced tea.

When Stephanie returned to Palmetto House late in the afternoon, she decided to press her red and white dress so she could wear it to the pops concert that evening. It took her twice as long as she had anticipated, and she was still at work on it when Lynne came in, pink-skinned and wilted.

"How was the game?" asked Stephanie.

Lynne collapsed on her bed fanning her face with her hand. "Great. He's a pretty good player."

"Who won?"

"He did. Actually I let him beat me," Lynne said, her smile colored at the edges with just a tint of mischief.

"Well, I guess that makes both of you feel good."

"He's a fanatic about tennis," Lynne said. "He wants to play again in the morning and then attend the play-offs in the afternoon at some racquet club."

Stephanie's plans for tomorrow—a long stint in the practice studio—suddenly seemed unbearably dull; and she wished fleetingly that she had something more interesting to do just this once.

After dinner, while Stephanie and Lynne waited downstairs in the lobby for Nick, who was going to the concert with them, Lynne suddenly exclaimed, "Stephanie, you look absolutely beautiful. You look like some mysterious, dark-eyed princess."

Stephanie laughed. She couldn't quite accept the princess part, but it was pleasing to hear. Lynne had offered her a drop or two of an exquisite perfume, and now its fragrance rose and fell around her like the breath of a hundred flowers.

Nick joined them, and they strolled down the boardwalk from Palmetto House to the Music Center, arriving early for the concert. They whiled away the time meandering through the adjacent seaside park as the setting sun filtered through a stand of tall pine trees and cast a rosy light on a festive scene. The park was filled with picnickers, and picnic smells were overwhelming. Aromas of pâtés and sausages spiced with garlic, onions and herbs swirled around their heads. The grape-rich bouquets of wines, their fragrances released as they warmed slightly, mingled with the familiar fragrance of fried chicken.

"Let's have a picnic next Saturday before the concert," suggested Nick, always ready to eat.

"Oh, let's," seconded Stephanie, wanting something pleasant to anticipate. "I love picnics."

In the lobby of the concert hall, small tables and chairs had been set up. White linen tablecloths and pink carnations created an elegant ambience. Waiters bustled about bearing trays of good-looking desserts made almost irresistible by glazed fruit decorations and clouds of whipped cream.

Having seated his two companions and maneuvered his own ample form into position, Nick, with a magnanimous air, announced, "The treat's on me this evening."

"Oh, thanks, Nick," responded Stephanie. She then realized that he hadn't heard her. He was beaming a smile at someone approaching from behind her. Glancing at Lynne she noticed a momentary cloud of concern in her friend's flower-blue eyes, then saw it give way to a smile, also. A small anxiety nudged Stephanie.

"Hello, Benedict. Come join us," Nick called heartily.

"Lynne, Stephanie, Nick." He greeted each warmly and bestowed smiles all around. With careless ease he grabbed the chair next to Stephanie and, after turning it around backward, straddled it as if it were a horse.

Stephanie struggled for composure. She hadn't counted on having to spend the evening in his presence. Of all the places out here he could have chosen, why did he take this one? She was intensely uncomfortable as yesterday's humiliation, unabated, flooded over her again, reducing her to yesterday's jittery schoolgirl.

Benedict turned to her. "I hope you're feeling better. Sorry you were down with a headache. I never have them, but I hear they can be annoying." His manner was pleasant and companionable.

"Yes, very annoying. I am better, thanks." Then she thought that this would be as good a time as any to thank him for the flowers.

"My pleasure," he replied, after she had said her simple "thank you."

"Benedict, that was a good article about you in the paper," said Nick.

"I think the reporter did a good job. He knows his business, and he kept his material straight. There were no surprises, and that's good. Sometimes I'm given quotes I hardly recognize. I'm lucky, because we got off to a bad start."

Stephanie shot him a quick glance, but to his credit, she thought, he kept his gaze on Nick.

"I agree with what you said about opera," commented Nick. "I, too, think it should be accessible to the ordinary music lover and not just to those with so-called high-brow tastes."

Suddenly forgetting her discomfort and her resolve, made minutes ago, to say as little as possible, she turned to Benedict and said, "You're surely not going to do it in English, are you?"

He looked at her in surprise for just a moment, then responded. "You make it sound worse than doing it in animated cartoons. No. You can relax. We'll do it in French, but I am thinking of super-titles in English. Actually I'm negotiating with the management about that now. You wouldn't object to super-titles, would you?"

Before she could gather her thoughts, a waiter appeared with a tray of desserts and gave a little speech about each. Lynne made her choice in about two seconds flat, and the waiter turned to Stephanie. She, unable to remember what he had said, couldn't make up her mind. It was a vexation to have to make decisions under Benedict's dark-eyed scrutiny.

"Nothing for me," she finally said.

"Stephanie!" It was a trio of reproaches.

"Well, anything, then. Anything will be fine." The waiter stood poised to deliver her choice. "Well, that," she said, pointing to a chocolate thing.

"Benedict?"

"No, thanks, Nick. I can't stay. I'm with that rowdy bunch right over there." He turned to indicate a table where Dave Hart, Phillip Downing, and several voice coaches appeared to be telling hilarious stories. Stephanie breathed out a discreet but thankful sigh of relief. "I just came over to have a word with this young lady, if you two will excuse me for a moment," he added.

Here it comes, thought Stephanie, stiffening as she remembered that he had requested a word yesterday in the Bon Appetit Sandwich Shoppe. While she held her breath waiting, he moved his chair in little four-legged hops so close to hers that their knees touched. This so unsettled her that she moved hers away as if she had been burned and at the same time turned to him with a stern look that was supposed to rebuke him for invading her territory. He acknowledged her scolding eyes with a guileless smile.

"You look nice this evening. Smell nice, too. I really like your perfume. What is it?"

"It's Lynne's. You'll have to ask her."

He leaned closer, and she made her chair hop away from his a mere inch or so, knowing that it was childish but unable to resist making a point. He followed her with a hop of his own. She hopped again, as did he. This is silly, she thought, so she stopped and slid over to the far side of her chair.

"Your move, Stephanie," he said, mischief in his eyes.

She glared at him. There were no more hops. He responded with an exaggerated expression of disappointment. Again he leaned toward her. Their fragrances mingled, her feminine one and his masculine one, and trembled in the warm air between them.

"Did you get my note?" he asked suddenly.

"Note?" she repeated, almost as if it were a new word.

"Yes, note. You got it, didn't you?"

"Don't talk so loud," she commanded in a sharp whisper, looking around to see if Lynne and Nick were listening. They weren't; they were happily engaged in an animated conversation of their own.

"I'll talk as I please," he said. "Now, about that note. I just wondered if you got it, since I didn't hear from you. It said 'urgent' and it was, or at least I thought it was. I waited all morning to hear from you."

"Oh. That's too bad. You shouldn't have," she said.

"But you did get it?"

"Yes, I did. About lunchtime, I think."

"I'm really curious about why you didn't respond. It seems to me that it would have been so easy to simply pick up the phone and say 'yes, thank you' or 'no, thank you'."

Everything he said was full of implied accusations that she had behaved badly, and now she was injured and defensive and close to losing her temper. She turned to look him full in the face.

"Benedict," she said, making an attempt to keep her voice even, "I haven't read your note. I'll read it tomorrow."

"You haven't read it!" he exclaimed, incredulous.

"I have not read it," she repeated. "I have had the worst migraine I have ever had in my entire life. It hurt to look at anything. And besides, I didn't much care whether it was urgent or not, since I was not in a position to do anything about it, anyway."

"Oh, Stephanie," he said, laying his hand on hers. "I am so sorry. I had no idea that you were so ill."

At the moment she moved her hand from under his, she noticed the absence of a wedding band on his ring finger, though she had absolutely no reason to care one way or the other.

"I'll read it tomorrow. I promise."

"Well, never mind. It's too late now," he said.

"If it's too late, why all this badgering?"

"Since I didn't hear from you, I wondered if you were in a fit of pique because of yesterday," he explained.

"You didn't hear from me because I had a headache, and I think that is a very good reason," she answered, a little curtly.

"Look, I didn't mean to harass you about this." He got up to go. "Take care." He touched her shoulder lightly. His hand left a hot spot.

"Benedict, hang on a minute," said Nick, suddenly realizing that he was leaving. "We're going to have a picnic next Saturday in the park before the concert. Why don't you join us?"

"He's probably too busy for such things," said Stephanie, looking at Nick with a small frown.

"Sounds great," said Benedict. "Thanks. I'll do it."

"I'll be in touch with you about who brings what," said Nick.

Stephanie watched Benedict make his way around tables, chairs and waiters back to his own group. Just before he reached his table, Dierdre suddenly appeared out of nowhere, it seemed to Stephanie, and called to him. He turned, and she rushed to catch up, talking and gesticulating all the while. They paused beside his table, he looking down into her face. Then Dierdre, apparently teasing, leaned against Benedict briefly in a provocative, intimate way. She said something. There was laughter, and they sat down.

Unable to turn her gaze from them, Stephanie was surprised at the sudden prickle of irritation she felt. Why should she care if Dierdre flirted with Benedict?

A few moments before eight o'clock the concert-goers streamed into the auditorium for the evening's program, an orchestral one. Nick sat between Stephanie and Lynne. Benedict and his friends sat several rows in front of them, Dierdre at his side. Stephanie, increasingly nettled, watched her whisper to him, saw him laugh with obvious pleasure and then lean close to whisper back into her red, crinkly hair.

When the concert was over, Stephanie, Lynne and Nick strolled through the soft night air back to Palmetto House. Although Stephanie could not remember one piece of music the orchestra had played, she agreed with her companions that it had been an evening of extraordinary music-making.

While the two roommates were preparing for bed, Lynne asked, "Are you feeling better about Benedict, now?"

"Not much."

"Why not? You two seemed to be having a nice chat. I thought him charming."

"It wasn't such a nice chat. All he wanted to know was why I haven't read his note. I've had better chats," replied Stephanie.

"Aren't you going to read it? Why don't you read it now?" Lynne could be as persistent as Benedict.

"He said it's too late now. It doesn't matter one way or the other," Stephanie said, picking up the envelope. She studied the handwriting, following each swing and loop of the thin black line as it formed her name. She imagined a masculine hand, tawny-skinned and strong, writing "Stephanie Morrison." Then she ripped open the envelope and withdrew the note.

Dear Stephanie,
I am willing to forget this afternoon's audition and start over. If you would like to have another go at it sometime tomorrow morning, please let me know tonight what time would be suitable for you so I can arrange my schedule and also make arrangements with Dave Hart.

Sincerely,
Benedict

All the humiliation of Friday's audition flooded over her again. Did Benedict Delman actually think she would willingly go through that ordeal again? It was about the last thing she wanted to do.

Lynne stood watching her, too polite to ask, but unable to hide the questions in her eyes.

"He wanted me to come for another audition," said Stephanie, and then read the note to her.

"I think that was very decent of him."

"Decent of him, yes, but his decency doesn't help me much. Even if I hadn't had a migraine, I don't think I could have done it. I hate turning in a performance that isn't perfect, it just absolutely tears me up. It was so embarrassing, Lynne, to go to pieces the way I did that I don't think I could sing for him now. My self-confidence has plummeted to zero, and I've got to build it back up."

"You probably didn't do as badly as you think you did. Don't be so hard on yourself. We're our own worst critics, you know."

"But I did so badly, Lynne. Benedict's note confirms it. The thing of it is I have worked so hard all my life, and I thought I was doing everything just right, so I simply don't understand why I made such a mess of it."

"It happens to all of us, Stephanie, one time or another."

"I know. It's just that I'm having a hard time with it right now." She drew a long breath and looked again at the note she was still holding. "Well, so much for Benedict's decency," she said, tearing the note to pieces and dropping them into the wastebasket. "Let's go to bed."

Sunday arrived, and Stephanie thought it was one of those extraordinary June days when it seemed that Mother Nature, in sweet contrition over her past indiscretions, went all out to charm and appease with a splendid array of good gifts. Stephanie, already dressed for breakfast, stood on their balcony waiting for Lynne, and surveyed the pale blue morning sky, the vast quiet ocean, pale, too, in the early sunlight, and the long stretch of golden-beige beach that yesterday had been so crowded with sunbathers. A little flock of sea gulls hovered in mid-air, curved wings outspread, then floated down to the water's edge like pieces of confetti. Such a beautiful blue and gold day! It called to her. To do what? She should go straight to the practice studio and put in a good day's work to make up for yesterday, that's what. The idea was as unappealing today as it had been yesterday.

"I'm ready, Stephanie," Lynne called, and they went downstairs to the dining room for breakfast. In a few moments Nick, then Hal joined them. Conversation was sporadic and subdued. A nervous anxiety, unspoken, showed in their faces; for after breakfast the cast for *Carmen* would be posted on the door of Rehearsal Room

B. Even though Stephanie was not expecting the role she had her heart set on—that was unrealistic—she was tense with dread. Long before she had finished her egg, her napkin was twisted into a rope.

Lynne and Hal left first. Stephanie ordered another cup of tea and sipped it slowly, in silence. Nick waited patiently as long as he could. Finally he said, "Well, shall we?"

"Shall we what?" she asked as if she didn't know.

"Go see who's going to be singing Don José."

"I suppose so. I'm dying to find out, but I dread going to see," she said.

"I don't think you have a thing to worry about," Nick assured her. "I've heard you sing, I know what you can do."

When they reached the Music Center, Stephanie put a hand on Nick's arm. "Would you mind if we sat down for just a few minutes? I feel a little jittery."

He looked at her with a surprised concern but said nothing as she led the way to one of the picnic benches in the adjacent park. They sat in silence for a few minutes.

"Nick."

"Yes, Stephanie. What is it?"

"Nick." Her voice was quavery. "You know that I haven't been quite myself since Friday."

"What is it?" He turned slightly to face her and, catching her hands in his, studied her with grave eyes. "You can tell me, Stephanie."

Dear Nick, she thought, though he was only twenty-six he sometimes gave comfort and counsel and invited confidences in just the way a wise and good mentor would.

"You'll find out in a few minutes," she said, "and I just want to prepare you for a big shock."

"Let's hear it, then."

"I'm not going to be Carmen," she said. "I know you have been thinking that I would play opposite your Don José. But I'm not, Nick." She turned her head away quickly to hide the tears in her eyes.

Finally he asked, "Why are you so sure?"

"I had a really bad day Friday, and I sang terribly, so I know I didn't get the part."

"You won't really know until you see the list. I can't believe you were that bad. Let's go have a look," he said.

Since she didn't get up right away, he pulled her to her feet, and she reluctantly followed him to Rehearsal Room B. A knot of hopefuls, all craning their necks to see, crowded in front of the door. Stephanie couldn't see one thing other than a T-shirt in front of her that asked in faded black letters, Have You Hugged Your Musician Today?

"Can you see, Nick?"

He stood on tiptoe, peering first this way then that, over and around the heads in front of him. In a moment or so he said, "You're right."

"Who is it, then?" Her heart was in her throat.

"Let's go," he said. "I don't know whether you want to hear this or not."

Not until they had left the building and were on the boardwalk headed toward Palmetto House did Stephanie ask, "Is it Lynne?"

"Yes."

"Don José? Is it you, Nick?"

"Yep," he said.

"I knew it! I knew it!" she cried, giving him a big hug. "You can go ahead and smile and yell 'whoopee' if you want to. I don't mind."

"I don't understand why you didn't get the part, Stephanie, bad day or not. What happened Friday?"

"Somebody upset me, and I lost control of myself."
After a moment or two she asked, "Who's Carmen's
understudy?"

"Dierdre."

"Dierdre! Dierdre Wellborn? Nick, are you sure?"

"Why does that surprise you so?" he asked.

"I don't know. No reason, I guess." Well, thought
Stephanie, the second audition paid off for Dierdre.

"Hal Piersen is Escamillo. He'll be sensational as the
toreador in a black wig and a curled mustache."

"Not even understudy," mused Stephanie, not paying
attention.

"Do you want to be understudy?"

"It's better than nothing. At least it would justify my
being here," she said. "Singing in the chorus isn't going
to do me any good. I can do that already. My career is
going to be at a standstill all summer."

Nick looked at her but said nothing. They walked in
silence until they reached the lobby of Palmetto House.
Usually she took the stairs, but today she waited with
Nick for the elevator. "I did so want to sing Carmen to
your Don José."

"I wanted it, too," he said. "This bad day business
really bothers me, Stephanie. You're such a tender thing.
We need to toughen you up, so the next time a bad day
comes along you don't go to pieces and sing off-key or
something."

When the elevator stopped at her floor she held the
door just long enough to say, "Maybe I'm just not ready
for St. Cecelia yet." Then she stepped out and stood
watching Nick until the door closed. Neither of them
smiled.

Disconsolately she trudged down the corridor to her
room, again wishing she had something more interesting

to do than practice her music. That was no way to spend a glorious Sunday in June. It would be lovely to simply jump into her car and drive through the country or go visit a friend. That was it! That's just what she would do.

Her college friend, Cyndi McConnell, who lived in Charleston, had invited her for a visit when she learned that Stephanie was to be in nearby St. Cecelia all summer. Stephanie had tentatively planned to go for the Fourth of July holiday, but she wouldn't wait that long. She would do it today. Charleston was only a short distance away; she could be up there in no time. First, she would telephone.

Cyndi was delighted, saying she couldn't wait to see her, and insisted that Stephanie spend the night and drive back in the morning. Quickly she packed a small overnight bag, scribbled a hasty note to Lynne, which she placed on her bedside table, and sprinted down the hall, her spirits rising with every minute. For some strange reason she happened to think about Benedict's note. Halfway down the hall, she slid to a stop and raced back to her room, where she dumped the contents of the wastebasket onto the floor. With quick fingers she fished out all the pieces of the note and tucked them into her tote bag. Somehow it didn't seem proper to allow the maid to cart it away as if it were nothing more than ordinary trash. Working fast, she scooped everything back into the basket and in no time was hurrying down the hall again. From the lobby she went out the side door to the parking lot where she had left her old gray Volkswagen upon arriving in St. Cecelia exactly a week ago.

Even though it was only nine-thirty, the roads were already clogged with lines of slow-moving traffic. It was not until she reached the wide open spaces of the causeway connecting the island to the mainland, with the hot, salty air stinging her face and blowing her hair, that she relaxed. In less than an hour she would be in Charleston.

Just a few miles before she reached her turnoff, she noticed in her rearview mirror a car driving fast and passing aggressively. Because she was maintaining a steady fifty-five miles per hour, it gained on her rapidly. She expected it to zoom past at any minute. Briefly she consulted her mirror again. A tailgater. Tailgaters made her nervous. She wished he would pass if he were in such a hurry. Instead of passing, he blew his horn at her. Of all the nerve. The left lane is open, sir, go to it. She looked into her mirror again, annoyed. There were two persons in the car. The horn blew again—short, repeated, demanding blasts. People can be so rude these days, she thought, especially in the anonymity of their cars.

When she looked again into her mirror, she saw that the passenger had stuck his arm out the window and was gesticulating for her to pull over. That made her even more nervous—and wary. They were up to no good. To stop would be naive, an invitation to trouble. She stepped on the accelerator just to put a little distance between them.

Just at that moment the car pulled out and shot up to a position parallel to hers. Frightened and wondering what she ought to do, she glanced quickly out her window and saw that Benedict was the mad driver, and it was Nick leaning out the window shouting to her and pointing to the shoulder. What now? she thought, hot with irritation. Then Benedict cut in front of her and began slowing down. At that moment she saw it in her rearview mirror: the blue light, spinning and flashing and bearing down on her. The police.

Just as she was pulling on her emergency brake, she saw that Benedict also had stopped a short distance down the road. Turning her attention back to the troubles at hand, she watched with mounting dismay as the young police officer strode toward her car with long-legged authority. She had never been stopped before. She expected the worst.

"May I see your driver's license, please?"

The temperature inside her car soared. Perspiration streamed down her forehead, ringed her neck, and dribbled off her elbows. She crawled out and stood to face him.

"Do you know what the speed limit is on South Carolina highways?"

Of course, she did.

"You were doing sixty-five. I'm going to have to give you a ticket," he said, almost apologetically.

"I know."

"I'd much rather give you a warning, but rules are rules. You know how it is."

"It's all right. I shouldn't have been speeding. I'll be more careful in the future," she said.

The officer took his time writing the ticket. Meanwhile Stephanie watched Benedict's warlike advance, with Nick somewhat in the rear. Looking up, the policeman caught sight of him and asked, "Oh, is this the boyfriend? He looks mad enough to bite nails."

Benedict, without a glance at Stephanie, marched straight up to the officer, held out his hand and declared, "I'll take that, if you please."

"I don't please. I'm going to give you one of your own. It's just as well you stopped. I radioed ahead to have you picked up. I clocked you doing seventy. You guys are in a real hurry today, aren't you?"

Nick arrived then, red-faced and puffing, and took his stand protectively beside Stephanie.

"I intend to take care of both tickets," announced Benedict in a voice that meant business.

"Indeed you will not. I'll take care of my own," said Stephanie, indignation in her voice.

"Well, I'll leave you two to straighten things out between you," said the policeman, giving both tickets to Benedict before returning to his cruiser.

Stephanie held her tongue until the policeman had driven away. Then, hands on hips, she addressed Benedict. "I was nice to that policeman, but I'm not so sure I'm going to be nice to you. I want to know what the meaning of this is."

"That's what I was going to ask you," said Benedict, unruffled by her ire. "Maybe you had better explain what you're up to."

"I'm not up to anything that needs explaining," she said. "I'm going to Charleston."

Benedict and Nick looked at each other.

"What did you think I was up to?" she demanded.

"I just happened to be looking out my window, and I saw you put a suitcase in your car and drive away," said Nick. He paused a moment to mop the perspiration from his brow.

Stephanie leaped into the temporary silence. "Is that any reason to hunt me down on the highway and scare me half to death? I didn't know who you were until you drove up beside me." She glared at Benedict. "And I still don't know what you had in mind."

"I think we ought to talk things out, Stephanie. That's what I had in mind," said Benedict.

"Well, I'm certainly not going to do it here. It's too hot, and I don't have time. Besides, I don't have anything to talk about, anyway. Give me my speeding ticket, and I'll be on my way," she said, holding out her hand.

"Look, Stephanie, I'm not willing to leave things this way. I don't think it's asking too much for you to take five or ten minutes to get this straightened out. You might consider the fact that Nick and I have driven twenty-five miles for that purpose."

"It was your idea, not mine," she said, "and, I might add, not much to your credit. However, I don't see why it has to be done this minute. Why can't it wait until next week?"

"Next week?" echoed Benedict and Nick in simultaneous surprise. Benedict recovered enough to ask, "When next week?"

"Anytime. I'll be back before classes tomorrow. Look, I've got to go. I promised my friend I'd be there by ten-thirty, and now I'm going to be late, thanks to you."

Benedict and Nick exchanged glances again, sheepish ones this time.

"Wait just a minute, Stephanie. It seems we owe you an explanation and an apology," said Benedict.

"You certainly do."

Benedict explained that when Nick had seen her drive away, he had sought out Benedict to tell him of her profound disappointment in not winning the role of Carmen. Her comment that singing in the chorus would do her no good and that her career would be at a standstill all summer led them to fear that she would yield to impulse and leave St. Cecelia without thinking things through. It was their concern for her that had prompted them to borrow Dave Hart's car and risk life and limb to chase her down. Obviously they were wrong in their conclusions, and for that they were sorry. Would she please accept their apologies?

When the explanations and apologies were ended, Stephanie got into her car, ready to leave. Benedict looked down at her through the open window. "Drive carefully. No more speeding. Fifty-five all the way. Understand?"

"Oh, glory," she muttered, and watched him begin the hike back to Dave's car. "Fifty-five, yourself."

After such an inauspicious beginning, the trip to Charleston and her visit with Cyndi and her parents turned out to be everything she had hoped for. Warm, loving, and high-spirited, they welcomed Stephanie immediately as one of them. In their presence it was impossible to nurse disappointments and mull over one's losses, and Stephanie drove back to St. Cecelia Monday morning refreshed and restored, completely satisfied with her Sunday outing.

Chapter Three

Monday, all morning long, Stephanie dreaded chorus rehearsal. To be relegated to the ranks of cigarette girl and gypsy was an affront to her. Besides, singing in a chorus wouldn't do one thing for her career. Her teachers had had high hopes and stern advice for her. "Stephanie," they had said, "don't settle for the chorus of even a major company and don't get stuck in minor roles. Go for the top. Never accept anything less, even if you're starving." She hoped fervently that none of them would ever hear of this summer's fiasco.

After lunch, feeling like a ninth grader who had been sent back to the eighth grade, she chose a seat in the back of Rehearsal Room B. She sat quietly, pretending to read the latest copy of *Opera News* and ignoring the chatter all around her as if to underscore the fact that she didn't belong there. She especially dreaded Benedict's appearance; she wished he wasn't working with them. He would only intensify her daily humiliation. Why couldn't he turn them over to a chorus master and save himself for the orchestra?

In a few moments he came striding in, charged with energy, followed by a more relaxed Dave Hart. Stephanie kept her nose in her magazine but listened intently as Benedict poured on the charm, chatting them up and getting them smiling. In no time he had them arranged into sections, ready for business.

"Now, sit up tall, back straight, feet flat on the floor," he instructed, "but I don't need to tell you people that, do I?" Stephanie, slouched out of view behind the mezzo-soprano in front of her, humored him by uncrossing her knees. The rest of the chorus inched forward in their chairs and pulled in their abdomens. After a careful warm-up, they sight-read through the choral music. "We're going to have a stellar chorus. You have a beautiful, warm, vibrant sound." His compliments rang with enthusiasm. "Thank you for a great rehearsal. See you tomorrow." The chorus responded with a tribute of applause. They would sing their hearts out for him.

Off and on, all during rehearsal, Stephanie had thought about her speeding ticket, which Benedict had failed to give to her yesterday. Now that practice was over, she had to get it from him. She would simply go up to him and ask for it.

She watched, waited for her moment, as half the chorus surged forward to surround him. It seemed everyone had something to say. She heard voices call out, "Great rehearsal, Benedict," or "Enjoyed it very much," or "You really put us through our paces," or "Good show." He seemed pleased and touched. As his last admirer turned to leave, Stephanie approached. He was still smiling, flushed with the pleasure of his success.

"When may I get my speeding ticket from you?"

At her abrupt question, his smile faded quickly. "Didn't you enjoy the music this afternoon?" he asked.

"It was enjoyable enough." She had enjoyed it enormously. "It just wasn't very challenging, I guess."

"I'm sorry you were bored. Here I was, expecting compliments from you."

"Oh, for heaven's sake, Benedict! Okay, it was a great rehearsal. Now, about that ticket."

"Thank you for your very kind words. Now, about that ticket." He made a big show of searching all his pockets. "I don't believe I have it on me right at the moment, and my schedule is so tight this week that I don't see any possibility of our getting together for a talk."

"I don't want to get together, and I don't need to talk. Could you bring it to dinner tonight and I'll pick it up then?"

He looked at his watch and started toward the door. "I hate to run off, but I've got another rehearsal in about two minutes. Take care."

Stephanie had another rehearsal, also. Those who had not won major roles in *Carmen* would participate in a series of Sunday matinees called "Introduction to the Opera." Working with their coaches, they would prepare a selection of scenes from a variety of operas and present them in concert version, without costumes or staging. Not too thrilling, but better than nothing.

When the first session ended two hours later, Stephanie had three assignments, two of them trouser roles—Hansel in Humperdinck's *Hansel and Gretel* and Octavian in Strauss's *Der Rosenkavalier*. She didn't mind singing the roles of young boys, but she had dreams of breaking into the musical world in a more spectacular fashion. In addition to the trouser roles, she would sing a scene from Mozart's *Cosi Fan Tutte*. She had plenty of work to do, enough to keep her from endlessly grieving over her lost Carmen.

Benedict, in spite of her urging, did not bring the speeding ticket to dinner. She would not give up. Later that evening, frustrated and more determined than ever, she decided to telephone him. Perched on the edge of her bed, Stephanie stared at the telephone. Seconds ticked away. Several times she wiped the palms of her hands down the length of her skirt, getting ready. Twice she dialed the wrong number before finishing the sequence. At last she heard his ring, sounding as if it were half a continent away. After that one ring, she hung up. What would she say to him now, after he had made such a point of ignoring her request? She wanted to present an argument that was both fluent and persuasive. While she thought about it, she sat watching the moist fingerprints fade from the receiver.

After walking around the room for a minute or two composing her speech, she brushed her teeth, drank a cup of water and returned to perch on the bed. This time, it would be do or die. Three rings. Thank goodness, he wasn't there. Enormously relieved, she had just started to hang up when she heard his "Hello?" She swallowed and tried to remember her opening words.

"Hello. Hello? Anybody there?" he inquired.

"Look," she began, finding her tongue. "Look, I want my speeding ticket." This was not what she had practiced.

"Oh, is this Stephanie? How are you?"

"Fine, thank you. Look, I still want that ticket. When can I get it?"

"You won't believe this, but I was just rushing out the door. Could we talk some other time?"

"I don't want to talk, I just want my ticket. Bring it to chorus tomorrow," she insisted.

"Thank you for reminding me about the ticket," he responded. "Please excuse me, now. I've got to run." With that, he hung up.

The next day when Benedict admitted that he had come to rehearsal without her speeding ticket, Stephanie wrote him a note requesting that he place it in the enclosed envelope and slip it under her door. The note came back marked, "Note returned to sender unread." All right, tit for tat. He had made his point.

She could be persistent. With a black magic marker, she printed her message: "Please enclose ticket in envelope provided." She left the paper unfolded, stapled an envelope to one corner, and slid it under his door. The answer came back: "NO!" Drat! What now? He was obviously holding out for a talk.

On Friday evening Stephanie was exhausted even before she went to the concert. It had been an especially hard week. In the gentle darkness with the music as soothing as a lullaby, twice she dozed off. Afterward, when Hal Piersen claimed Lynne for late-night dancing at Salamander's, Stephanie decided to call it a day.

Alone at her door, she couldn't find her key. She even turned the contents of her tote bag out on the floor before she was convinced that she didn't have it. It was eleven o'clock. The office downstairs would be closed. There was nothing to do but wait for Lynne. Heaven only knew how long she would be out. Until the wee hours, probably.

Stephanie blew out a big sigh and slumped against the wall. Well, this was no place to wait. Dragging herself down to the lobby, she collapsed in one of the chairs beside a green growing thing with leaves entirely too shiny.

Restless because the chair was not very comfortable, she grew more annoyed by the minute and finally went out into the clear, starry night.

Twice around the square she marched, fired up by frustration, before following one of the little crosswalks to the statue of St. Cecelia gleaming in the moonlight. The statue stood in the middle of a large round pool. Stephanie climbed over the petunias to perch on the rim. The blossoms surrounded her with their achingly sweet scent, intensified in the warm night air. Four little fountains splashed the surface of the water with silver spangles. Lovely.

She put her chin down on her updrawn knees and gave herself over to the hypnotic dance of the moonlit waters. After a while the sound of approaching footsteps, ringing with a hollow sound across the square, intruded upon her reverie. She would remain still, pretend ignorance of their approach. Carefully she risked a peek. Benedict. He stopped at the edge of the petunias. She didn't look up.

"What are you doing here in the middle of the night?" he asked.

"Wishing somebody would give me my speeding ticket."

"Oh, that. Can we talk?"

"Now? Look, I've told you all week I don't want to talk."

"I'm serious, Stephanie. Can we talk?"

"You just did."

"Don't be difficult. You know what I mean."

"All right. We'll try. You go first. What do you want to say?"

He hopped over the petunias and sat down, facing her. She looked straight into his eyes.

"For pure unadulterated fractiousness, you take the prize," he said.

Stephanie blinked once but didn't turn her eyes from his. "Well, I certainly got that one."

Silence. Stephanie thought they were like two cats on a fence in the moonlight, standing eye to eye.

Finally she said, "If the conversation is over, I think I'll go sit somewhere else." She swung her feet down right into the petunias.

"You're squashing those crape myrtles."

"They're petunias," she corrected, with prim authority.

He laughed. "Oh, Stephanie, you're too much. Come on. I want to talk to you, but first I have something for you. Let's go."

Ah-hah! The speeding ticket. It's about time.

When they entered the lobby Benedict headed straight for the elevator and pushed the Up button. A wariness that had been growing in her suddenly ballooned when he said, "I'm on the third floor."

"Wait a minute. Where are we going to do this?"

"My room. Isn't that all right?"

"Are you crazy? This time of night?"

"Oh, don't be a schoolgirl, Stephanie." He paused, looking at her. "Well, your room then. Would you feel better in your room?" he asked, holding the elevator door.

"Not much, but we can't get into my room. I can't find my key, so I'm locked out until Lynne comes. Besides, it's her room, too. What about right here in the lobby?"

"This is no place to talk. Come on."

They went up to his floor, and while waiting for him to unlock his door, she said, "I don't know why I'm doing this."

"Maybe we can talk about it someday," he replied with an easy smile, gesturing for her to enter.

Even though his room was exactly like hers, it felt different. Its very maleness made her intensely aware of him. In the middle of the floor between the two beds sat a pair of his shoes draped with gray socks rolled inside-out. Coming upon his shoes like this, she was suddenly startled by the real essence of him. He saw her looking and kicked them under the bed. On the dresser were colognes and lotions, in dark green or blue bottles with silver or gold-colored trims and tassels. In the nearby closet hung shirts, jackets, and trousers, some with belts dangling from their loops. Scattered about the room and completely covering the lamp table were musical scores, books and a multitude of notes on yellow lined paper.

"I'm going to make us some tea," he said, filling a small electric kettle with water. He set it on the dresser and plugged it in. "I don't believe in going to rehearsals unprepared, so I'm often up until all hours doing my homework. A cup of tea keeps me awake. Got in the habit in England, I guess." He smiled at her. "The tea's there in that box, Stephanie," he said as the water began a thumping, roaring boil. "And here's a cup." He slid a tall, gray-blue speckled mug down the counter toward her.

"Watch out, this water's really hot," he warned, getting ready to pour it into her mug.

"Would you be more comfortable on the bed or in the chair?" Benedict asked, steaming mug in hand.

Stephanie laughed. "The chair's fine."

Benedict, after setting his tea down on one of the notepads, reached into a drawer. "This is for you," he said, handing her a long, slender parcel.

She looked at him in surprise. It was not the speeding ticket. "What is it?"

"Open it and see." He was watching her intently.

Under his scrutiny, she worked at it with little success and increasing agitation. Finally, as though he had just remembered it, he took from his pocket a tiny gold knife and slit the stiff brown sealing tape. At last with trembling hands, she peeled off the paper. The opened box revealed its mystery—a tomato-red umbrella with Metropolitan Opera printed in white block letters along one of its ribs.

"Oh, my goodness!" She was overwhelmed with a confusion of emotions. "How did you get it so soon?" she asked, trying to sail past the realization that she was deeply touched.

"I have a friend in New York. I called her last Friday night and said I was desperate, could she help me? She could and did."

"I bet she wondered why you were so desperate to have this very umbrella, of all things." Stephanie was fishing. Had he told his friend what had happened?

"Well, I think she was a little curious. I told her the weather down here was terrible and getting worse by the minute." Stephanie read accusation in his eyes. He regarded her with such an intensity that she bristled slightly.

"Don't look at me. I'm not responsible for the bad weather down here," she said, returning the look with an intensity that matched his.

"You were there, too, remember?"

"Not by my own design," she protested, "and, if you remember, hardly in a position to direct the weather."

"I admit you were in an unfortunate position, but that didn't keep you from messing up the whole scene. If you had cooperated, I think we might have managed without mishap."

"Wait a minute," she said, "I'm confused. I thought, for just a minute, that you were going to apologize, but now it seems it was all my fault. I'm afraid I don't have an apology ready."

"You don't need to get one ready. All that is ever necessary is a simple 'I'm sorry', but I'm not asking you for one. I'm trying to make one myself. I thought the least I could do would be to replace your umbrella and say that I really am sorry."

The very least, she thought.

"I'm sure you could say a great many things about what happened last Friday," he continued. "I'll admit that my behavior was unconscionable. After you had said you didn't want to get your shoes wet, I should have left you alone. I know that now."

"You certainly should have. Why didn't you?"

"You were irresistible, I guess. You looked so beautiful standing there all in red that I really did want to pick you up and carry you off." He smiled at her as if he hadn't entirely given up the idea.

The compliment found a home in Stephanie's heart. She began to soften toward him a little.

"Also," he added, "I think I saw myself as some gallant hero saving a maiden in distress. I was as surprised as you must have been that something that started out so innocently ended so badly. I'm terribly sorry."

"You're right, it did end badly," she agreed. "It ruined my whole summer."

"Oh, come now. It wasn't that bad. Besides, it's only the second week of June."

"It is *that* bad. I had my heart set on singing Carmen. I didn't get it because I sang badly. I know that, but I wouldn't have sung badly if you had minded your own business that morning.''

"I see," he said, looking at her gravely. "Would it make you feel better to know that we chose Lynne, not because you were so bad, but because she was so good? She is exceptional, Stephanie."

"Maybe some other people are, too. Maybe me, for instance. You don't know about me."

"Since I'm under attack, I would like to point out that I went to some pains to give you another chance. That's what I wanted to speak to you about in the sandwich shop, but you wouldn't listen. And, according to your own admission, you didn't even read the note I sent. I don't know what else I could have done."

"If I had come, would it have made any difference at all? Could you have judged me fairly?"

"Of course I could have judged you fairly," he said, with a little show of indignation, "and I did judge you fairly. I was afraid you might think I hadn't. That's why I wanted to give you another chance. As I said, we chose Lynne because she had everything we were looking for. I have a lot at stake here. This *Carmen* will be my debut as an opera conductor, so naturally I wanted to assemble the very best cast possible." After a brief pause, he went on in a gentler tone, "Part of being professional, Stephanie, is knowing where your limitations are."

"Limitations!" she cried, incensed. "I don't think about limitations. If I did, I would never get anywhere. You think about them, though, don't you? I get the feeling that you think I'm pretty limited." When it looked as if he would remonstrate, she insisted, "Well, you do, don't you?"

"What do you want me to say? Obviously you do have potential. After all, you were chosen from a field of six hundred applicants to come here, but, just as obviously, you are young and inexperienced. You don't have control of yourself yet. How old are you, anyway?''

"Thirty," she lied with a little show of defiance.

Benedict laughed. "I'd guess closer to thirteen. Now, don't get in a huff. I think you're charming, whether you're thirteen or thirty. And you're bound to improve with age," he said with just the flicker of a smile.

"I knew it," she said, half in banter. "You think I'm terrible."

"Are you?"

"I must seem so to you, though I'd not noticed it myself until last Friday."

"Oh, I think you're probably worth saving," he said.

"Your appraisal gives me faint courage. Nick thinks I'm wonderful," she said, smiling. "He never mentions my limitations, and he's never once accused me of being thirteen."

"I know," he replied. "You have done a real snow job on Nick. He keeps trying to tell me that you're not half as terrible as I think you are."

"I certainly hope you improve with age, too," said Stephanie.

Benedict laughed. Then she looked at her watch, surprised at how late it had grown. "Oh, my. Look what time it is. I'd better go." Getting to her feet, she added, "Children my age should be in bed."

He stood to face her. "I wish you wouldn't. Thirty-year-olds can stay out all night if they want to. If you insist, though, let's make certain everything is clear between us. I know you won't be able to forget what has happened—I know I won't—but maybe you can move it to some remote corner of your mind so you won't see red every time you see me. Will you try?''

"I'm not ready to yet. One more thing. I want my speeding ticket."

"You know, I've never seen anyone in my whole life so eager to have a speeding ticket."

She held out her hand. "Never mind. The ticket, please."

He came toward her. "Stephanie, Stephanie, there is no speeding ticket. It's all taken care of. Days ago. Forget it."

"How much was it, then? Tell me and I'll write a check."

"You shouldn't ask people how much they paid for things, now should you?"

His question made her feel about thirteen years old, but she persisted. "This is different."

"No, it isn't. I don't want you to pay me. I want to do it for you. It's all right. Let it be."

"I feel funny about it, Benedict. I don't like it."

"Don't worry. Are we ready for the truce?"

"I don't know. What are the terms?"

"Cessation of hostilities and the initiation of friendly overtures," he said smiling. Then he gave her a quick, chaste kiss on the lips. "Like this."

"Oh," she said, putting her hand to her mouth and stepping back in surprise.

"I startled you, didn't I? I won't do it again," he said, pulling her to him. "I'm giving you fair warning."

"Oh, no." She was breathless.

"Oh, yes." His arms closed around her, and his dark eyes brooded over her face. She tried to defend herself against their spell and held out for the space of three or four breaths. The room grew warm; the embrace, warmer still.

He kissed her eyes, her cheeks, the tip of her nose, and teased her lips with soft, little pulling kisses. Once, his hand stroked down the length of her back, rounded her hip, and came back up, evoking strange awakenings. She could hardly bear the sharp ecstasy of it, and then his lips were on hers in earnest. Someone moaned. The room whirled. Stephanie forgot to breathe.

Alarmed at the gathering force of his passion and her own unprecedented response to it, she pushed frantically against his chest. His lips released hers, slowly, reluctantly. He laid his cheek against hers.

"Oh, Stephanie. Dear, feisty Stephanie," he murmured.

She drew away abruptly. "Feisty?"

"Shh." Then, cheek to cheek as they were before, she gave herself up to the ineffable sweetness of his embrace. A lovely warmth stole all through her body, melting away the last vestiges of the hostilities she had nursed all week. Gone, also, was the terrible exhaustion of the early evening, and she grew tipsy on the scent lingering on his skin. There was wonderful stuff in those blue and green bottles on his counter.

After they had regained their equilibrium, he walked her to her room. On the way, she said, "Thanks for the tea and the umbrella, but you really shouldn't have done it."

"The tea or the umbrella?"

"The umbrella."

"It was worth it. What about the speeding ticket? Do I get a thank-you for that, too?"

"I suppose so, but you shouldn't have done that, either."

"It was worth every penny. I'd do it again with pleasure. If you ever get another, let me know."

"You're crazy."

"So are you. It's catching." He kissed her again and they both laughed for no reason at all.

Outside her door, they stood smiling at each other for the longest time. When Lynne's voice responded to her soft knock, he kissed her quickly and left.

Still drifting earthward from cloud-high euphoria, Stephanie stood in the middle of the room, enjoying the descent. Squinting and blinking, Lynne scrutinized her roommate.

"What has happened, Stephanie? You look as if you have just discovered champagne."

Softly her feet touched down, but there was music in her heart. Arms outstretched, she swirled into a spin, then dropped onto her bed with a big, happy sigh. "Not champagne. Earl Grey tea, and it's beyond anything."

Chapter Four

In spite of snatching only a few hours' sleep, Stephanie awoke Saturday morning in a buoyant mood. It was just the sort of day to encourage high spirits. The sky was clear, the sea sparkled, and a fresh little breeze whipped up a scattering of whitecaps in the ocean. She began counting the hours until the picnic.

At six o'clock that evening, the four friends arrived in the park and discovered that all the tables had already been claimed. They chose a spot in the shade and set down their glossy, violet shopping bags from Bon Appetite Caterers.

"This isn't going to work," said Stephanie, frustrated at the sea-scented rambunctious breeze that seemed determined to get something started with their red-checked paper tablecloth. "Everyone grab a corner and sit on it. I guess we'll have to tuck our napkins under our chins to keep them from blowing away."

"Curried rice salad," announced Nick, busy empty-
ing one of the purple bags. "Here's lemon chicken. This
must be the marinated vegetables. Lynne, look in the
other bag and get the melon and prosciutto. We'll start
with that. Benedict, you be the wine steward."

"Aren't we elegant? Look, stemmed wineglasses in
pure plastic," said Benedict, handing them around, his
uncorking duties completed.

"Nick wouldn't hear of paper cups. I was going to save
us some money," said Stephanie.

They drank to the success of *Carmen*, to their health,
to their futures, to the French Revolution and finally to
finish the bottle.

"Clean your plate, Lynne, or no dessert for you,"
urged Nick.

"I couldn't possibly eat another bite," said Lynne.
"What's dessert?"

"You just barely missed having imported fresh figs at
ten dollars a pound," said Stephanie, laughing. "You
ought to try shopping with Nick sometime. He could
spend a fortune for one meal and not blink an eye."

"You just ought to try shopping with a tight-fisted
penny-pincher. Our Stephanie here is going to make some
lucky husband the ultimate frugal housewife. Just think,
forty years of married bliss and a steady diet of econom-
ical beans and rice," said Nick.

"Well, hardly. I probably won't marry, so that lucky
man can eat lobster with somebody else."

"Not going to marry! Why not?" This came from
Benedict.

"Why does that surprise you? I should think you, of
all people, would understand," said Stephanie. "Didn't
I read in the newspaper that you, yourself, believe a
musical career and a marriage won't work?"

"You make it sound worse than it actually was. I said that it's a rare marriage that could survive the stresses and strains of the constant travel and the frequent separations," explained Benedict. "I hope you didn't make that drastic decision based on what I said in that interview. I'll have to be more careful about what I say in the future. I'd hate to think I'd driven a beautiful woman like you to a nunnery."

"Not the nunnery, Benedict. Rome, Paris, London, Munich, or wherever. And I do think you overrate the power of your pronouncements. I make my decisions based on my own counsel, thank you."

"Lynne, how do you stand on this?" asked Benedict. "Are you going to sacrifice wedded bliss for a career?"

"I don't think so. I want it both ways, I guess. I'll take everything life has to offer—a career, a husband and family, a house in the country, a couple of horses, a dog, a canary or two." She ended up laughing at her list.

"Oh, Lynne, how can you possibly take on all that without making compromises? As for me, my wants are simple. I ask of life just one thing," said Stephanie.

"Well?" Benedict looked at her with that strange intensity in his dark, gypsy eyes that she had seen before.

"To make it to the Met—as a star, of course. That is my one and only dream."

"You'll make it, Stephanie, I know you will," said Nick.

"But you don't think you can do it with a husband in tow?" asked Benedict.

"Well," she retorted, "you, yourself, in that well-quoted interview, said that you were too busy with your career right now to think about marriage. Apparently a wife is just as much a hindrance as a husband is."

"How did we get off on marriage? I thought we were going to have dessert," said Nick, reaching into the bag for a bowl of strawberries. "Aren't they beauties?"

"Ah, strawberries and wine!" said Benedict, choosing a huge berry, bursting with ripeness and red as a ruby. Holding it by its little green cap, he dipped it into his wine, touched it to Stephanie's lips, then popped it into his own mouth.

"Oh, you!" she cried.

He chewed it slowly, closing his eyes in exaggerated ecstasy. After a moment he peeked to see if she was watching.

"Now, this one is for you," he said, dipping another. A drop of wine clung to its point, shimmering. He dangled the strawberry seductively right under her nose. It looked luscious. Each time she started to bite it, he moved it ever so slightly toward his own mouth. She knew what he was going to do. It was a sneaky way to steal a kiss.

"You've got this all backward," she said. "It was Eve who tempted Adam. Not the other way around." Immediately she knew she shouldn't have said it.

"So it was. I'll gladly yield if you want to be the seducer, but I thought you were a little slow in getting started." He brushed the strawberry lightly across her lips again. "Do you want to seduce me?"

"You're a naughty boy. I'll give you a strawberry if you want one, but—and I'm afraid you'll find me very dull—I don't do seductions."

"Maybe you'll change your mind." Here he gave her the strawberry. "Actually I didn't start out with the idea of seducing or being seduced. I believe you brought that up, but it doesn't sound like a bad idea. Maybe we ought to talk about it sometime. I don't believe it's covered under the terms of our truce.''

Stephanie thought that Lynne and Nick watched the entire absurdity with exactly the right attitude. It was understood that things that happen at picnics shouldn't be taken seriously.

''A glorious repast,'' said Nick.

Wonderful strawberries, thought Stephanie.

All around them, picnickers were beginning to shake out their tablecloths and repack their baskets. The magic spell was broken; the picnic, over. Already groups of people were drifting through the mellow evening toward the Music Center.

''We'd better start cleaning up,'' said Stephanie, ''or we're going to be the last ones here.''

''No sooner said than done,'' declared Benedict, springing suddenly to action.

In a few moments they, too, sauntered from the park toward the Music Center, Stephanie and Benedict hand in hand and casting long shadows in the last rosy light from the sun.

When the lights dimmed inside the concert hall, the music lovers settled themselves into their seats and waited for the conductor. Benedict leaned toward Stephanie to say that this conductor, a young Brazilian, had received rave reviews so far on his North American tour. That news, though interesting, did not have quite the effect on Stephanie as the touching of their shoulders when Benedict whispered in her ear.

The conductor appeared and bowed, the applause died, and the orchestra began. Stephanie's shoulder burned. She began to wonder if Benedict was going to sit through the entire symphony leaning against her. She tried hard to concentrate on the music, but what she heard was Benedict's quick, shallow breathing. Back to the music.

Every now and then she could feel his empathetic participation as his muscles tensed and he, almost imperceptibly, leaned into the down beats. Sometimes he stretched up tall in his seat to see what was going on among the cellos or the woodwinds. Two or three times he frowned, and Stephanie wondered what had displeased him. Once he said "Ha!" under his breath and smiled, and she surmised that the violins had executed some particularly difficult passage with precision and grace.

Then her gaze fixed on his hand, resting palm down on his program. It was the sort of hand she had seen in advertisements for men's prestigious watches. The neat, well-cared-for hand of a man who has made it to the top and who is knowledgeable about the finer things of life in a casual sort of way. She imagined his hands and hers—small and delicate beside his—playing piano duets all through some dreamy summer afternoon. The windows would be open to the green, gently rolling countryside, and the sheer, white curtains would billow in the breeze.

Stephanie shifted slightly in her seat, leaving an infinitesimal space between them. He turned to look at her briefly, the lustrous eyes filled with music. He drew her arm back so that it rested against his, just as before.

She sighed softly and yet again tried to concentrate on the music. The young Brazilian was stabbing the air in a frenzy, his hair in wild disarray. The orchestra was working up to a hair-raising finish. The exquisite tension exploded in a roar as the audience jumped to its feet, crying bravos. Benedict was among the most enthusiastic. Stephanie rose, too, clapping hard but never turning her eyes from him.

"Bravo, bravo!" shouted Benedict. He leaned close to announce his appraisal. "World class, absolutely. What do you think?"

"World class," she responded, applauding all the more enthusiastically.

Later, after the two roommates returned to their room, Stephanie slipped out of her red shoes and climbed up onto her bed, still dreamy-eyed.

"What have you done to Benedict? Or should I ask, what has he done to you?" Lynne asked. "I couldn't believe my eyes tonight."

"Nothing to both questions, other than what I told you about the umbrella and the apology. He's just being nice, that's all, and I'm trying to live up to my end of the bargain. Our truce, you know."

"Truce, fiddlesticks! I don't think I saw white flags in his eyes when he looked at you tonight. It was more like a purple passion."

"Oh, Lynne, that's ridiculous," she said, suddenly engrossed in inspecting her nails.

"Did you think that little seduction-with-a-strawberry bit was prompted by peace-keeping motives? You two were so cute. While watching it, I didn't get the feeling that it had anything at all to do with the cessation of hostilities, as you put it. I think he's smitten, Stephanie."

"I doubt it," she said modestly. Nevertheless she felt pleased and twittery.

On Sunday morning after she and Lynne returned from a pre-breakfast run on the beach, Stephanie dressed with unusual care. Rather than jumping into just any old pair of clean shorts, she put on a new azalea pink cotton sundress, piped with white. Her favorite color, it always made her happy. She fastened a string of little white beads around her neck and felt very dressed up. A bit fancy for the practice studio perhaps, but it was Sunday. When she was a little girl, she had always loved Sundays, because she could wear her prettiest clothes, and her grandmother always made a big fuss over how nice she looked. A pleasant memory, it made her smile. She leaned toward the mirror, her lips taut, ready for the raspberry gloss that she held in her hand. This morning she wasn't dressing for grandmother.

It all paid off. In the dining room, Benedict came straight to the table she shared with Lynne and Nick, and sat down beside her. "Thought I'd check and see if the truce is still working," he said in a low voice, leaning close in a drift of mint and the heady scent of his cologne. "You look nice this morning. That dress is just the color of crape myrtles. Pretty."

"Azaleas," she corrected with prim sweetness, pleased that he noticed.

They were about halfway through their bacon and eggs when Hal Piersen joined them to claim Lynne for another morning of tennis.

"Do you play, Stephanie?" asked Benedict.

"Sorry, I don't. You'd better ask Nick."

"Sorry, I don't," Nick answered. "They don't make tennis shorts in my size. Besides, I hate hitting things, except, of course, high notes."

"I wish I could play. It looks like a great game," said Stephanie.

"If you want to, we can bat a few this morning," offered Benedict.

"No, really. You'd be bored to death. I've never had a racket in my hand. I don't even know what love is."

They all laughed. Then Benedict said, "Well, for starters, there's puppy." More laughter.

"And erotic," added Hal.

"Brotherly and sisterly," Lynne chimed in.

"Courtly." This was from Benedict who, to illustrate, gave a flourish with his hand.

"Platonic," said Nick.

"True," offered Lynne.

"Thank you all very much. This has helped a lot, but I still can't play. I've got tons of work to do today," said Stephanie.

"Why are you going to work today?" asked Benedict. "Lynne's not working, Nick's not, Hal's not, and I'm not, either."

"I have to. I'm a workaholic."

"Nonsense," said Benedict. "You need to take time off for fun and games. It's good for you."

"Benedict's right," said Nick. "There's more to life than just music."

"Didn't I read just a week ago that a certain someone said that music is a demanding mistress?" asked Stephanie, looking at Benedict.

"So she is, but she takes Sundays off," he explained.

"Well, all right, for a little while." She really did need to practice, but she also wanted to be with Benedict. Feeling somewhat guilty, she promised herself she'd work twice as hard during the afternoon.

A little while later Stephanie, in white shorts, her hair in a ponytail, stepped onto a tennis court for the first time in her life. Squinting up at Benedict under a cloudless, blue sky, she repeated, "You're going to be bored to death. Really, in about five minutes, you'll be sorry you ever mentioned this. Shouldn't we just take a walk? Or maybe we could watch Lynne and Hal."

"I'm not going to let you back out. Relax, you're going to enjoy it, and so will I. Now, first, the grip," said Benedict, holding his racket straight out in front of him. "See where my thumb is."

"I may not be too good at this."

"You're going to be wonderful. Don't worry."

To inspect her grip, he hovered very close behind her. Placing his hand on hers, he made repeated adjustments, sighting along their extended arms. She found it difficult to concentrate. Finally, stepping away from him, she said, "I can practice this later, let's just hit the ball to each other." She felt strangely breathless.

"You'll need the swing for that. This is the forehand," he said, demonstrating several times in slow motion. It looked perfectly simple. "It feels like this." Again, he stepped behind her. They touched from shoulder to knee, and from her shoulder to knee there flashed a bolt of lightning.

Grasping her hand on the racket, he made their two arms swing as one. "Back up and over," his voiced intoned. "Did you feel the follow-through?" he asked.

"Follow-through? Uh, oh, yes. I mean, no. No, I didn't feel anything like that. Let's just practice with the ball."

"You didn't feel anything?" He was incredulous. "We'll do it again." After completing several more swings, he inquired, "How was that?"

"I don't know. It's hard to tell when you do it for me. Let me do it by myself." He stepped back to watch, and an acute attack of self-consciousness struck her. With him looking at her that way, she'd never get it right. Relax, she reminded herself, and instantly tightened her grip on the racket.

"Now, don't forget to shift your weight," he cautioned from behind her again. "Like this." His left arm encircled her waist and pulled her against him. Awareness left her brain and strung itself out along the length of her back. "See how your weight shifts to the forward foot as you reach the top of your swing and begin the follow-through?"

Weight shifts from forward foot.... She tried to impress that upon her befuddled brain while one foot—was it the forward?—wanted to run for dear life and the other realized that a simple pivot would place her cheek to cheek within his arms.

"When can I hit the ball?"

"In a minute," he replied, continuing to shift weight until he was breathing hard.

Finally Stephanie, breathless herself, broke away and said, trying hard to keep her voice steady, "I think I'm ready to hit the ball, now."

"All right, but first, about love. You were interested in love, I believe."

"Not anymore. Love's premature at this point. I'd rather play. Come on. Throw me the ball and I'll hit it back to you."

"Love has to do with scoring," he continued in the we-will-carry-on-no-matter-what voice of one who has been instructing recalcitrant pupils for decades.

"I don't care about scoring. Let's play." Running to the other side of the net, she bent her knees in a half squat, her racket at the ready. "Okay," she called.

She saw him toss the ball into the air and heard him thwack it hard. There was a whoosh. She swung wildly.

"Not so hard," she yelled.

"You have to keep your eyes on the ball."

"How could I? I never even saw it," she complained.

"Here comes a nice slow one," he promised.

"Drat! I missed that one, too."

"Don't look at me. Keep your eyes on the ball from the minute it leaves my racket."

So he instructed, but her eyes persisted in looking at him while the balls whizzed past her right shoulder. Her teeth clenched, her knuckles white, she attacked fiercely. The harder she tried, the more frustrated she became. His very patience was disconcerting. Why did she let him rattle her so? He was absolutely right the other day when he said that she didn't have control of herself yet, but she felt sure she could master this whole game in no time at all with any other instructor. With Benedict, she had managed to hit only three of all those balls and none of the three had gone over the net.

"You're wearing yourself out," he called. "Let's take a break." He came around to her side of the net and began gathering up the balls. She collapsed on the grass in the shade. He dropped down beside her and said, "Your face is as red as a beet and you're soaking wet." He pulled out a handkerchief. "You stay here and mop up, and I'll go find us something to drink."

When he returned with two soft drinks, she said, "Tennis is a lot harder than I thought it would be."

"What's the problem?"

What could she say? You upset me? Hardly. "I break concentration. It's too hot."

"You seem uptight to me. I think you're trying too hard. Can't you relax and just enjoy it?"

"Not really. I keep thinking that you expect me to be wonderful, and I'm not wonderful, so I get tense."

"You *are* wonderful. You're doing fine. You just need to loosen up a bit." He took a long drink from his can. "So... I make you nervous."

That wasn't precisely true, but she didn't correct it. What she had said was not completely so, either, but it had served better than the absolute truth. How unlike her to hedge and equivocate.

"Anything else? Was the instruction clear? Am I going too fast?" He set his drink down between his feet and looked at her, all attention, his eyes troubled. "Okay, let's hear it. What's bothering you?"

She returned his look, considering. What could she say? Your eyes. The way you kissed me the other night. Your hands on mine. The way you look in that white polo shirt. Your little white shorts. The way you serve the ball. She said, "I'm just naturally a tense person."

"Well, we'll just play it loose and easy. Tell yourself it doesn't matter whether you're wonderful or not. It's just a game, and games are to enjoy." He pulled her to her feet. "Ready? Let's hit a few more."

She felt better now, calmer. Maybe she could hold her concentration and really hit them this time.

When they re-entered the court, Benedict said, "I think you're ready for love now." He took her racket and the can of balls she was holding and put them down on the green pavement beside his. Something in his voice and manner made her wary. What was he up to? She decided on a straightforward course. She would get right to the point.

"It has to do with scoring, hasn't it?"

"Right. I'll show you. First, courtly." With a flourish, he bent low from the waist, took her hand and placed a chaste kiss on the back of it. "Very suitable for the courts," he explained, mischief glinting in his eyes.

"Benedict!" She had barely recovered from the sudden change in mood when he announced, "Platonic," and kissed her briefly on the forehead. "Brotherly and sisterly" brought her two innocent little pecks, one on each cheek.

"Clown," she accused, smiling. "Let's play."

"And, now, puppy," he sang out, continuing down the list. He caught her in his arms and began nibbling and nipping under her chin and all around her neck from one ear to the other, all the while accompanying his energetic explorations with playful little snuffling and growling sounds. He was very good at it.

Stephanie giggled and squealed, "Stop, stop. No more puppy!" But the more she squealed and struggled, the more rambunctious he became and the more she laughed. Finally he got so tickled at himself that they both ended up clinging to each other, laughing almost to the edge of collapse.

When he had recovered enough to speak, he announced with a certain fervor, "Now, the final point in my lesson. Erotic." Little gold flames flickered in his eyes. His face glowed with mischievous, eager energy. She knew what was coming.

"Oh, no, not here, Benedict!" She broke free and backed away.

"If not here, where?"

He was going to pounce any moment. She looked around wildly.

"Over there!" She pointed to the azalea bushes just outside the court and darted in their direction, with Benedict in pursuit. From there, she sprinted to a clump of palmettos, barely escaping capture. Again she yelled, "Over there," and pointing left to a stand of tall Yucca grass, ran in the opposite direction to take refuge behind the trunk of a huge live oak. She listened for pounding feet. Hearing nothing but the wind rattling the nearby palms and the singing of the birds, she risked a peek and found herself face to face with her pursuer, who was stealthily creeping around the tree. After a display of resistance, she allowed herself to be caught. Benedict put enough into the kiss to make the chase worthwhile. The lesson, received smoking-hot from his lips, was still flaming on hers as they sauntered back to the court to pick up their gear.

A strange exhilaration surged through her. She picked up her racket, and on impulse, tossed a ball high into the air. With spontaneous exuberance, she swatted at it. She felt the thwack—right in the sweet spot. The ball rose in a beautiful arc right over the net and flew higher and higher until it disappeared out of sight over the fence.

Ecstatic, she let out a gleeful whoop. "Oh, did you see that? Right over the net! I did it! I did it! Wasn't that wonderful?"

"Where did it go?" asked Benedict.

From beyond the bushes in the direction of the swimming pool came a man's voice, "Where in thunder did this tennis ball come from?"

"All the way to the swimming pool! Wasn't that wonderful, Benedict?" She was about to explode with triumph.

"Yes, really wonderful, but it wasn't wonderful tennis. A referee would call that 'Outside.' You need control."

"Oh. You're no fun at all," she accused in a pretended pout, but she couldn't remember when she had had such a good time.

Chapter Five

Late Monday afternoon Stephanie slumped at the piano in the practice studio, staring at the *Carmen* score, which was opened to the cigarette girls' chorus. She hadn't made a sound for five minutes. Her voice trailed off and finally stopped right in the middle of a phrase. Her left hand still held down a chord that had, some moments before, died of old age.

This gypsy music had magical, evocative powers, but they weren't working right this afternoon. By now she should have been transported, as a cigarette girl, to a square in old Seville. In her imagination she had gotten only as far as Benedict's room in Palmetto House, and had lingered, lost in his arms. There, she might have stayed all afternoon, had not the picnic floated into focus and then faded into that crazy, whimsical tennis lesson. She touched her cheek, where, on Friday night, his evening beard had made even stubble look and feel sensational, and sighed.

On impulse, she turned her score to the "Habañera," Carmen's song. Something about it—its lilting melody or its words, as familiar to her now as her own name—called to her irresistibly. She had to sing it, just this once, then get back to work on the chorus music.

"Love is a child of the gypsies," she sang, and then poured her whole soul into the repeated *amours*. The word, like a magical invocation, called up the image of Benedict's face, his dark eyes burning with that intensity she knew so well.

Then the word "love" seemed to explode into a cascade of shining stars. Love? Stunned, Stephanie stopped mid-phrase. Love? Oh, no! That's utterly ridiculous! It can't be, after only two weeks and two kisses. It just doesn't happen that fast except in books and movies, and she hadn't expected it to happen at all. It was not a part of her plan. Maybe she was jumping to conclusions. After all, wasn't it still true, in spite of that tennis lesson, that she didn't know a thing about love?

She knew about crushes, though. She had had one once. Perhaps years from now, she and Benedict would meet again—she, a world famous opera singer and he, an internationally renowned conductor. They would be sipping an aperitif in the half light of some enchanting Parisian café, and she, with a charming little laugh would touch him lightly on the arm and admit that once, years ago, that summer in St. Cecelia—did he remember?—she had had a crush on him. Perhaps it would be a poignant moment for both of them.

She shifted her weight on the hard piano bench and sighed again, almost overcome by the bitter sweetness of her romantic reverie.

"Love is a child of the gypsies," sang Stephanie again.
"He's never known any law." A mere crush, she told
herself and closed the book.

That evening at dinner, freshly showered and lightly
perfumed, she could barely wait for Benedict's arrival.
She expected him to come straight to their table. He
would lean close and give his usual compliment, the
blandest one in the world, "You look nice." Tonight he
might add, "Smell nice, too. Is that fragrance crape
myrtle?" She would correct him with a prim smile.

All during the meal he would scarcely know what he
was eating. Under the table, their feet would touch, ac-
cidentally at first, then deliberately seek each other out.
With their eyes they would send secret messages, and
Lynne and Nick would never suspect a thing. She
watched the doorway with an anticipation that grew
sweeter by the minute.

When finally he arrived, trailed by Phillip Downing
and two other men, each of them carrying manila fold-
ers, Stephanie's heart sank. Disappointment settled in as
she watched them, looking very serious and business-
like, head for a table in the far corner of the dining room.
Obviously they were deeply engrossed in some conversation that had started earlier in another setting. How
different this Benedict was from the one who had given
her a tennis lesson yesterday. This one seemed a stranger
to her. She had expected yesterday's Benedict, who would
have, by now, at least discovered her presence and sent
her a smile across the room. She watched and waited and
eventually left with Lynne and Nick, feeling dissatisfied.

After dinner she went back to the practice studio, but
she might just as well have sat on the beach. Something
was wrong with her brain. It refused to operate on all but
one channel, and that one channel did nothing but flash

images of Benedict. What was she going to do? She had to memorize the chorus part soon. She sighed. Well, tomorrow she would pull herself together and attack it in earnest.

During the following week when Benedict joined them at breakfast or dinner, Stephanie soaked up his smiles, marveled at his wit and stored away in her memory new impressions of him for her romantic reveries. Every sighting of him, however brief, set off in her a sunburst of pleasure. She lived for chorus rehearsal each afternoon when she could look at him to her heart's delight for two solid hours. Never had she seen anyone like him. Never had anyone affected her so. Never had she had so much difficulty keeping her mind on her work. By the end of the week, she was close to panic because she was so far behind. She would absolutely have to shut herself up in the practice studio all Saturday afternoon and the entire day Sunday to catch up.

Consequently Saturday morning at breakfast when Benedict asked, "Ready for a tennis lesson this afternoon?" she replied with brave resolve, "I'd love to, but I really must work."

"Not today, Stephanie. I won't take 'no' for an answer. I've been very good and let you work all week. It's time to play, now." His eyes were irresistible.

After only a little persuasion, she relented and then even agreed to go to the concert that evening with him. She'd work all day tomorrow.

Breakfast on Sunday, however, led to more tennis. And tennis led to lunch, which, somehow, led to an agreement to spend the afternoon touring the island on bicycles, even though she protested, "I haven't ridden a bike in years. I'll probably fall off and break my neck."

They walked hand in hand to the bicycle rental shop. Excited and a little apprehensive, Stephanie stood beside Benedict and surveyed the lineup of bicycles.

"That blue one there looks pretty good, Stephanie. Why don't you try it?" he said.

She made a rather wobbly test ride and quickly confirmed his appraisal while he tried out several before settling on a silver one.

Bicycles chosen, they went outside and studied the map, standing so close their shoulders touched.

"Let's take this route across the island to the sound," suggested Benedict, running his finger along the black line. "We can visit Snug Harbor, then come back around the tip and ride down the beach. We can stop for a swim anywhere along here. Is that all right with you?"

"Sounds wonderful. Hope the old legs hold out."

"Since you haven't ridden in a long time, we'll take it easy. You just let me know if you get tired."

Benedict took the lead down asphalt paths skirting centuries-old live oaks festooned with Spanish moss, which looked to Stephanie like grizzled beards hung out to dry. Once her initial insecurities about riding were overcome, the pair whizzed past pine and palm trees and petunias, marigolds and zinnias planted along the boulevards, at the edge of the woods and around the traffic circle as well. Weathered villas set in exquisitely manicured parks, lined their route. Every time they came upon a lagoon, Benedict insisted that they stop. "Let's look for alligators," he'd say, peering into the inky water.

"This water's so black, we'd never see one."

Several times they saw egrets standing in the shallows on long, fragile legs, the white of their bodies in sharp contrast to the dark water.

"How do they stay so clean?" wondered Benedict. "One dip, and they'd be ruined forever."

"Obviously they don't dip. You'd never catch them in up to their ears. They wade in only ankle deep. That's why they're not ruined forever."

"Your legs holding up okay, Stephanie?"

"Fine and dandy," she answered, not about to admit being close to collapse.

Most of the time he maintained a pace that kept her breathing hard and pumping steadily. Every now and then, when the path was straight and clear, he lowered his head and surged ahead in a great burst of speed and then came pedaling back to her, his face glowing.

By the time they reached Snug Harbor, Stephanie was barely able to pedal. Benedict parked his bike in a rack and came bounding to the curb where she had stopped.

"I believe an iced tea would do you good," he said, lifting her bike up onto the sidewalk. "Then a brisk walk around the harbor will get the kinks out of our legs."

"Nothing brisk, please," she said, hardly able to move.

"Legs tired?"

"No. Legs are fine. I slowed down so I could watch for crape myrtles," she said, too weary to smile. Her thighs burned, her calves were bunched into knots, and her knees refused to straighten.

"You're walking a little funny. Why didn't you tell me you were tired? We could've stopped any time. It's perfectly all right to admit you're tired, Stephanie."

"I didn't want you to think I was a weakling and couldn't keep up."

"You thought I was expecting you to be wonderful. Is that it?"

"I guess so."

"Well, I don't expect wonderful people to wear themselves out. I'm going to have to take better care of you," he said, smiling at her. Then they started toward the snack shop. Crouched under a dense canopy of enormous oaks, a string of little gray-shingled cottages connected to one another by a long front porch beckoned to Stephanie and Benedict.

"This must be the prototype of modern shopping malls," said Benedict as they waded through dark, gray sand to mount the wooden steps. "It has everything you need when you've already got everything. Would you like one of these orange St. Cecelia T-shirts? Or how about one of these fuzzy pink monkeys?"

Next door to Island Crafts, which displayed a variety of baskets woven with sea grass or wild grape vines, was Naturally Yours, a snack bar. They entered and sat down at a tiny square table covered in yellow and orange flowered vinyl. A smudgy chalkboard advertised the daily special: Three Alarm Chili.

Waiting for their orders, they held hands across the vinyl, his thumb caressing the back of her wrist. Then they chatted over their tea and ice cream, pistachio for her and chocolate for him.

"Do you come from a musical family, Benedict?"

"My mother is very musical. She plays the piano. Still practices every day. Her first love was singing, though. She was just getting started in a very promising career when she met my father. They married, and babies began appearing at a rather alarming rate, but she never complained or hinted at regrets."

"I bet there are not very many women now who would give up a promising career so easily," observed Stephanie.

"I wonder if she would, if she were making the choice now instead of thirty years ago," said Benedict.

"Though I wouldn't do what she did, I'm glad she did what she did," said Stephanie, smiling and reaching across the table to touch his hand briefly.

"Does that mean you're finally starting to like me?" Benedict asked, his eyes glinting.

"Well, we have become good friends," she admitted.

"Very."

"Do you suppose your mother has ever regretted it?"

"When she was young, women were expected to marry and have families. A career was something you had until you found a husband, or if you couldn't find one. I think she did what seemed to her at the time to be the right thing. As for sacrificing so much, she has certainly given every appearance of being perfectly happy and fulfilled. She has made all of us feel that we were very special, very precious gifts. I've loved her since I first set eyes on her."

"How many of you are there?" Stephanie asked.

"Seven. Five boys and two girls."

"Good heavens! I don't see how she found the time to practice the piano every day. Are all of you musical?"

"My poor mother tried valiantly to make us so," Benedict replied. "We all took lessons of one sort or another and gave lots of recitals for our long-suffering relatives and friends, who seemed to think we were terribly charming all dressed alike in our little white sailor outfits. But I'm the only one who's stuck with it. I think I'm more like my mother than any of the others, and I guess, deep down, I feel as if I should sort of pay her back for what she gave up for us."

Stephanie couldn't help smiling at the thought of Benedict in a little white sailor suit. What an adorable child

he must have been with a headful of dark curly hair and
those lustrous dark eyes!

"What about you?" he was asking.

"I have one brother, and I'm the musical oddity in my
family," she said. "Whatever musical ability I have has
come by way of hard work, not genes. In fact, my mother
doesn't have any faith in music at all. She keeps urging
me to take business courses, just in case. If I were to turn
into the first vice president of something she would be
very pleased."

"Why doesn't she like music?" Benedict wanted to
know.

"Oh, she likes it, but not as a career for me. It's not
practical, and she's very practical and very realistic. She's
had to be. My father left us when I was ten, so she had to
work. She's a school teacher."

"It must have been very hard on a ten-year-old," observed Benedict, "to divide your time and your loyalties
between your two parents."

"Actually I haven't seen my father since he left. Now
I don't much want to. It's obvious he doesn't care. Why
should I? But I guess I do, a little."

"Poor Stephanie."

"No, it's all right. Really." She gave him a weak smile.

"How does music figure in with all this trauma?" he
asked.

"Well, I'd started piano lessons when I was seven, and
by the time I turned ten, I was playing rather well. I enjoyed it. That summer, Mother sent my brother and me
away to stay with our grandparents. She was actually
going to school to get her teaching certificate renewed,
but I thought she was abandoning us. I just knew that
we'd never see her again. As so many children of divorc-
ing parents do, I thought that we were the cause of their

trouble. I was miserable with guilt and despair, so I took refuge at the piano. I sat there and cried and played for hours, day after day. I don't know how my grandmother stood me that summer, but she was really great. I remember having these terrible nightmares and waking up terrified half to death, and she would come and hold me until I went back to sleep again. Anyway, to make a long, sad story short, music became my father, my friends, my whole life, really."

"But you did go back to your mother at the end of the summer?"

"Oh, yes. With great relief, I must say."

"After becoming so involved with the piano, why did you turn to singing?" Benedict asked.

"My friend coerced me into trying out for the glee club in high school because she was afraid to go by herself. Ironically I made it and she didn't. Anyway, I discovered I had a voice, and it just started to blossom, to the delight of my teacher and the despair of my mother. I, of course, wanted to start taking voice lessons, and Mother said would I please tell her where the money was coming from. I said not to worry, I would work and pay for my own lessons. I worked on the weekends and during the summers all during the rest of high school."

Benedict enclosed her hand between his and pressed it warmly. "You are an astonishing young woman."

"Not really. It isn't astonishing or unusual to work for what you want. I'm determined to make music work for me because I have so much invested in it. Besides, I love it. It still is my whole life. You understand that, don't you?"

"Yes, it's that way with me, too."

Later, hand in hand, they strolled down to the harbor, where boats bobbed at anchor around a circular inlet. On a point of land, a lighthouse stood guard, a black and white sentinel with a nautical gift shop at its base. Stuccoed villas with turrets and balconies overlooked the water. Between the houses, arches with black wrought-iron gates gave alluring glimpses of flowering courtyards where, underneath those colorful umbrellas, beautiful people undoubtedly lived the good life. Stephanie imagined herself, a famous singer, as guest of honor in such a setting as one of these.

Benedict, though, was more interested in looking at the boats than at the houses. They followed the sidewalk from the lighthouse all the way around the inlet to the opposite side, stopping to gaze a long time at each craft, every one a dazzling white in the brilliant sunlight.

"Oh, look! There's *Miss Prudence* and there's *My Last Love*," cried Stephanie.

"I'll take the *Hesperus*," said Benedict, looking with great longing at a sailboat that seemed to Stephanie to be about the size of the *Queen Elizabeth II*. It rocked rhythmically in the water, its halyard pinging against its mast. "Boy, oh boy, wouldn't I love to own that little baby!"

"Would you really? What on earth would you do with it?" She turned to him, suddenly incredulous.

"Think, Stephanie. What would you do with it?"

"I wouldn't do anything with it. I wouldn't have it in the first place," she assured him.

"You wouldn't? Why?"

"I wouldn't have time to enjoy it, and I don't see how you would, either. The more successful and famous you become, the less time you'll have. Most of your life, you're going to be in some hotel thousands of miles away."

"It's going to be that bad, huh? Why are we in this business if we can't have boats?" he asked.

"Because we love it, that's why. Music is in our blood. But we both know that musicians don't live normal lives."

"I don't know that at all. Ascetics don't make very good musicians."

"I'm not talking about asceticism," she said.

"What are you talking about, then?"

"Well, I'm just wondering why a musician caught up in the demands of a career would be willing to spread himself so thin with boats and things," she said.

"Lots of people with careers have boats and manage very well. What's the problem?"

"A musical career is different. The problem with having a boat is the same as having anything else that ties you down, like a house filled with priceless antiques or a family of a dozen children. What I'm saying, Benedict, is that people and things make claims on you."

"That's the way it should be. I don't want a life with no boat to sail in or no house to come home to or no one in it when I do arrive from wherever. Especially people. I could never give up people, not even to be the most famous conductor in the world. I need to belong to people and have them belong to me. Don't you, too, Stephanie?"

"You yourself said that marriage and a musical career won't work. That's giving up people," she pointed out.

"I think I said it would be a rare marriage that could survive, and there are some rare and beautiful marriages in this business. I know some of them. I wish you could meet my friends, Celia and Loren Carruthers. They're both singers, and they would restore your faith in love and marriage." He smiled down at her, obviously re-

membering them with fondness, then turned to look at
the boats in silence for a while.

After a few moments and in a much lighter vein, he
said, "Well, at least a boat won't cry or cheat on you or
divorce you if you stay away too long. I intend to have a
boat. Maybe I'll take you out for a sail someday just to
keep your routine of nothing but music from turning you
sour."

"I'll probably be singing at La Scala on that day," she
said.

"Do you mean to tell me that you would actually turn
down a sailing date with me just to sing at La Scala?" he
asked with feigned incredulity.

"Well, I'd have to see the boat first."

"I knew I could tempt you." He laughed and gave her
a quick, playful hug. "I have a better idea. Why don't I
rent a sailboat next Sunday? Would you like that?" His
eyes were shining with excitement.

"Oh, my, yes! I'd love it. I've never been sailing."

"Great. We'll do it, then. Before the day's over, you're
going to want a sailboat, too. Wait and see," he promised.

When Benedict had had enough of looking at the boats
and they had mounted their bikes again, Stephanie discovered that her legs remembered every turn of the ped-
als that had brought them to Snug Harbor. They still had
a mile or so to cover before reaching the tip of the island
where they could finally nose their bicycles southward
and head for home. Already, she was looking forward to
the swim, if for no other reason than to rest her weary
legs.

At the tip of the island, they left the shaded path for
the sunlit shore, riding close to the water's edge where the
sand was wet and firm. They dodged toddlers with pails,

by-passed sand castles, zigzagged around Frisbee games and joggers, and set sea gulls whirling and sandpipers skittering.

"This is marvelous," called Stephanie, skimming along the beach, her hair flying, her cheeks stinging in the salty sea breeze and her eyes filled with the shimmering dazzle of sand, sea and sky.

"Legs holding up okay?" shouted Benedict over his shoulder.

"So far, so good."

"Want to stop for a swim or go on?"

"Swim!" she cried, ready to collapse.

As they parked their bikes side by side in the sand, she was suddenly stricken by a wave of self-consciousness. She wished she didn't have to take off her shirt and shorts. She knew he would look at her, in that appraising way, and it would probably make her blush. Shoving her hands into her pockets, she turned away and waited for him to make the first move.

"Are you going to swim in that?" he asked.

"I could," she replied, briefly considering it.

"Don't you have a swimsuit?"

"Yes," she said, turning to look at him. "I've got it on."

"Shall we, then?" he asked, unbuckling his belt.

She kicked off her sandals, first right, then left, stalling.

Then, following his lead, she unzipped her shorts and let them slide down her legs. With unnecessary care, she folded them, painstakingly matching seams and creases, and laid them on her bike seat, just so. He, with exaggerated carelessness, simply hooked his on the toe of his shoe, kicked them up, caught them with his hand, and flung them in the general direction of his bike. She wanted to taunt him with "Show off," but couldn't.

Sea gulls circled. A feisty breeze whipped her hair across her face and flirted with her shirttail. Her fingers fumbled with her top button as she watched him, cross-armed, pull his knit polo shirt over his head and toss it wrong side out to where his shorts had landed. Trying not to stare, she bent her attention to her second button, but her hand loitered there. His little swimming trunks were black.

"What a slowpoke!" he said, stepping close and reaching for her third button. The air suddenly seemed charged. As his hand moved to her fifth and final button, her eyes caught the rapid, rhythmic pulse of his heartbeat in the hollow of his throat, and she realized that her own heart was keeping time with his.

Just as he pushed her shirt from her shoulders, she pulled in her abdomen and held her breath. The shirt slithered down her arms and fell past her hips to lie unnoticed in the sand. The sun instantly warmed her bare skin, his eyes warmed it even more. She forgot her abdomen. Each movement had seemed deliberate, played out in slow motion, heavy with significance. Was this the way newlyweds felt undressing together that first night?

"You look nice," he said, as she knew he would. His compliments never varied. "That's a pretty color. Crape myrtle, isn't it?"

"Hot pink."

"No wonder I'm sizzling." He grinned, obviously trying for a light touch. She looked up and gave him a squinty smile through her billowing hair. They both looked away for a moment, then back into each other's eyes. The light touch wasn't working.

"Oh, Stephanie," His voice was low, hushed. In one impetuous move, his arms enfolded her, snuggling her so close that she felt the accelerating thud-thud-thud of his heartbeat. Or was it hers?

Tense and expectant, she waited. His breathing grew quavery and ragged, and at the end of a long, roughly drawn breath, his lips suddenly possessed hers. Then, just when Stephanie felt she couldn't endure the exquisite agony a moment longer, the kiss ended as abruptly as it had begun, its passion not spent, merely suspended.

He uttered some fierce, inarticulate cry, broke from her, and started running across the sand toward the surf. Dazed, Stephanie stood swaying in the sunlight, her hands pressed to her burning lips. Some moments passed before she halfway regained her composure, but when she finally did, she noticed. He still had his shoes on.

"Benedict, your shoes!"

He was knee-deep and still running. He dived into a wave, which collapsed over him in frothy disarray. A few seconds later she saw his head pop up. He swam a few strokes, then started toward her, streaming water. She splashed out to meet him, calling, "Your shoes, Benedict. Your shoes."

"What? What about them?"

She pointed to his feet, the shoes now clearly visible through the ankle-deep water.

"Ah! They were new," he howled, holding up one dripping foot to view the sodden shoe.

"I guess they still are. But don't you worry. They will dry and be as good as new."

He looked at her as if startled at this unexpected and familiar reassurance, then began to laugh. He wrapped his cool, wet arms around her, and they clung together laughing wildly, not altogether because the wet shoes were so funny.

When she could finally speak again, Stephanie said, "You know, I have the feeling that we are being carried right out to sea."

"We do get carried away, don't we?"

"I mean, the waves rush by us so fast and furiously it feels as if something is pulling us in deeper and deeper. And the sand, it's really weird, but it feels as if it shifts right under my very feet and falls away, so that I have to keep going farther in to have something to stand on." She looked down at the swirling water, green in the sunlight. "See, we're up to our knees already."

Chapter Six

On Monday afternoon as Stephanie was leaving chorus rehearsal, Benedict called to her to wait. When at last they were alone, he said, "How about another tennis lesson tonight after dinner?"

"Oh, Benedict, I'd really love to, but I just can't. I've got to work. I've promised myself I'd work until ten o'clock every night this week."

"Good heavens! What for?"

"So I can go sailing with you on Sunday. I'm really looking forward to that. It sounds so exciting, I can hardly wait. But I can't play tennis and go sailing all in one week."

Benedict removed his music from the conductor's stand and slipped it inside a battered, brown leather briefcase. "I think you go at it too hard, Stephanie. You don't need to work every minute of every day."

"You don't understand. I've got to. I hate not being perfect."

"Life is more than being a perfect musician. You can't live on music alone."

"I can."

"Well, I can't, and you shouldn't. You need to develop other skills and other interests—you'll be a better musician if you do. At the rate you're going, you'll burn yourself out before you reach your prime."

"That's what Nick tells me."

"Why don't you pay attention to us wise guys, then?"

"But I'm so far behind, it drives me crazy. I didn't get much done last week."

"All right. Tell you what—you work until ten, then go swimming with me. I'll meet you in the lobby at fifteen after."

"Benedict Delman, you're a bad influence on me, but it does sound tempting. Maybe I will. It will be my reward for working extra hard tonight." A moonlight swim—she'd always dreamed of it. Would it be as romantic as she had imagined it? A delicious anticipation had already begun to blossom inside her when, a moment later, she and Benedict parted and dashed off to their next assignments.

After dinner, humming a merry little tune and barely suppressing a jig, she hurried to the practice studio, her arms full of music and her head full of moonlight swimming. Even at the piano the watery images persisted until she was at the point of gritting her teeth in an attempt to concentrate. She would stare at the music and make the right sounds, but suddenly, Carmen's world would fade from her mind's eye and in its place she would see two figures, pale in the moonlight, standing close in an embrace, up to their waists in shimmering dark water, its surface strewn with flower petals, rocking gently.

With a start at a faint noise from somewhere, she returned to the business at hand. She attacked her music with a renewed determination. Still every fifteen minutes she consulted her watch and heaved exaggerated sighs at the ploddingly slow passing of time. Would ten o'clock never come? Finally, right on the hour, she charged to the inn to change for her swim.

Wrapped in terry robes and carrying towels, she and Benedict went out into the summer night. It was going to be better than she had imagined it. She was prickly with anticipation. The pool court, illuminated by lights high in the palms, was deserted except for a mockingbird pouring rhapsodies from a nearby rooftop.

"Wouldn't you love to be able to sing like that?" asked Benedict, slipping out of his sandals.

"I can. I'm a coloratura mezzo, so his little trills and embellishments are a piece of cake for me," she said.

Benedict's sudden look of wide-eyed incredulity gave her a flush of pleasure. "That's a rare bird," he said.

"Are you surprised?"

"Obviously I can't say yes, but I honestly can't say no, either. I'd like to hear you sometime."

"You already have." She was surprised at how flat her voice sounded.

"Can't you forget that?"

"Wish I could." She turned away to look again at the mockingbird, but it, apparently startled, stopped mid-song and flew away. Stephanie saw it only as a brief flash of white.

A breeze, busy for a moment among the palm fronds, blew across to visit the pines, then lingered among the petunias long enough to gather their sweet scents and swirl them around Stephanie's head like a perfumed veil. It lifted the edge of Benedict's towel, shook the hibiscus, and then rippled the pool, clear as an aquamarine, setting its surface shimmering.

"What a beautiful night!" said Stephanie softly, deliberately putting away the disturbing memories of their first meeting and trying to reestablish the dreamlike atmosphere of her fantasies. She removed her robe as if it were a gossamer cape encrusted with pearls.

Benedict ripped his off and flung it down on one of the plastic lounge chairs. "I really need this," he said. "It's been a long, hard day." He stood poised on the edge of the pool for a moment, then sliced through the water in a beautiful, clean dive. With vigorous strokes, he swam down to the end of the pool.

On the return lap he came over to where she still stood, high and dry, and raised his arms to take her into the water. Squatting, she rested her hands on his shoulders. Suddenly he plopped over backward, yelling "Whee!" and carried her with him. They made a big splash, and the frothy water closed over them.

Then came the incredibly delicious sensation of floating on top of him in a tangle of cool, slippery arms and legs. It lasted only a moment, and it was lovely getting untangled and clinging to each other, still sputtering. The water lapped endlessly against their bodies in soft, rhythmic caresses. His lips were cool.

Suddenly he released her and, turning away, began swimming briskly, leaving shattered reflections and scattered bubbles and sparkles in his wake. She watched him for a few moments, then stretched out into a lazy crawl. She loved the sensation of gliding through the silky water, feeling graceful and weightless, her hair swirling around her head like a scarf.

She had swum several laps when she saw Benedict do a string of somersaults, then come gliding up to her under water. He grasped her ankles and pulled her down to him. He pressed his lips to hers and then swam away. Later, they became playful and perfectly at home in the water, rolling and turning and gliding with curving, sinuous movements. They swam over, under and around each other, meeting and parting. They floated side by side on their backs, rising and falling together in the gently lapping water. A star-studded velvet blue sky canopied their watery Eden.

After a little while Benedict stood up and asked, "Had enough?"

"No," Stephanie said with a sigh. "This is so lovely, I wish it could go on forever." She touched bottom and stood up. Then, quite suddenly, he lifted her half out of the water and, to her surprise, pressed a kiss in the little hollow between her breasts.

"I've been wanting to do that all evening," he said. "You are so beautiful."

Afterward, as they walked along the beach hand in hand, she could still feel the prickly stubble of his beard against the swell of her bosom.

They strolled in silence for a while, then Benedict asked, "Where are you going to be this fall?"

"Lyric opera in Chicago." She had received a letter confirming this only a few days ago but couldn't bring herself to tell him then.

"That's great," he said, but he didn't sound pleased. "What about you?"

"New York. Associate conductor at the Met."

"That's wonderful," she said, suddenly heartsick.

"We're the lucky ones, I guess."

"Yes, very lucky," she agreed over a huge lump in her throat.

"You know what would be fun?" He draped an arm across her shoulder. "We should plan to meet here, just the two of us, next June for a little reunion. Would you come?"

"Oh, yes. I'd love it," she agreed.

"Let's say the first week of June, then. Be sure to write that down on your calendar," he said.

"I bet we don't make it. If you were to get an invitation to go to Vienna, you'd cancel us, wouldn't you?" she asked, looking at him intently.

"Would you?"

"No, of course not," she answered, stoutly.

"Why do you think I would?"

"I don't know. Your career. I just wondered."

"Well, we'll just say that this comes first and plan our schedules around it. If we have to, we can move it a few days one way or the other. I suppose it would be better to be somewhat flexible. The important thing, though, is to get together," he said.

Long after she was in bed that night, Stephanie thought about the distant rendezvous with increasing perturbation. That Benedict would suggest such a thing implied that, in his view at least, their relationship was not to be continued beyond the summer, but, instead, renewed next year for a few days. Why was this disturbing to her? Hadn't she insisted all along to her mother, her friends, as well as herself, that music, and only music, was the life for her? Weren't men a distraction and marriage, well, wasn't marriage an outrageous impossibility? The answer was a hearty, unequivocal yes. Why, then, couldn't she accept their present relationship for what it obviously was—a summer romance—and enjoy it on its own terms?

On Thursday night when they met for their swim,
Stephanie thought Benedict somewhat preoccupied, and
she assumed that some unsolved problem from the day's
work was pressing him. He would be himself again after
their frolic in the pool, she was sure. But he dived in immediately and began swimming fiercely non-stop. He
churned the water to a fine froth with his powerful arms
and legs, as if bent on total exhaustion.

Feeling abandoned, Stephanie went to the far side of
the pool to keep out of his way, and disconsolately swam
her laps.

While they were drying themselves, she was unable to
keep quiet any longer, and asked, "Is something wrong,
Benedict?"

"Why?" He was drying his foot. He didn't look up.

"You attacked the water as if it were your enemy, and
you've worn yourself to a frazzle. Besides, you've hardly
spoken to me all evening. Have I done something to make
you angry?"

"No, no, you haven't." His reply was testy. "Work's
getting to me, I guess. That's all."

"Do you want to talk about it?"

"No, I don't." He slapped at the glass-topped table
with his wet towel and turned to look at her. "But I guess
I've got to. Ready?" He draped his towel around his neck
and headed off in the darkness toward the beach, leaving her to follow, puzzled at his behavior.

They walked some distance in silence before he said, "I
know you're going to be upset when I say what I've got
to say."

"I've been upset for the last twenty minutes wondering what's wrong with you," she admitted.

"I got a telephone call today from a friend of mine
who plays cello in the New Horizons String Quartet.

They're scheduled to play a quintet with piano in Washington this Sunday afternoon."

Why should that be upsetting? she wondered, then said, "Oh. You want to go hear them."

"Not exactly. The problem is that the pianist broke his collarbone in an accident last night, and now, of course, he can't play. Since I've played this piece with them twice before, they want me to fly up tomorrow evening to be there for a Saturday rehearsal and to play with them on Sunday." He looked at her for a long time for that to sink in.

"Oh. So that means we can't go sailing on Sunday," she said. "Is that what I'm going to be upset about?"

"Well, I told them I'd already rented a sailboat, but that I'd talk to you. I know you've been working hard all week just so you could go, and I know you'd be terribly disappointed if we called it off."

"But what about a pianist for the quintet?"

"They'll have to find somebody else. No problem."

"Then why are you telling me all this, if there's no problem?" she asked, bristling a little.

"I thought that since you were involved, you should know," he said.

"What do you expect me to say? Do what you want to do."

"Well, I hate to disappoint you."

"I'll probably get over it. The real problem is that you don't want to be responsible for breaking our date."

"No, I don't, but that's not the point. The point is that this is a crisis, and we can go sailing any time."

"Did you really think I would fling a fit and insist on sailing? Wouldn't sailing be fun under those circumstances?"

"Well, I thought—I hoped you might be more gracious about it," he said.

"I think I might have been if you had simply said, 'Stephanie, I'm sorry I'm going to have to disappoint you.' Then I would have said exactly what you wanted me to say, and I would have been very sweet about it."

"I've handled this all wrong, haven't I?"

"You underestimate me, Benedict."

"You misunderstand me. My main concern was not, as you supposed, to spare myself guilt, but to avoid disappointing you. I was ready to put you first, because that is what I really want to do."

"Well, I am disappointed, but I would be more than disappointed if you didn't go help out your friends." She heard a sigh of relief in the darkness beside her.

"Stephanie, I really didn't want this to come between us. Can you believe that?" His voice was tender.

"Yes, I can, but you know as well as I do, Benedict, that music will always come between us. It's that way with music."

"You're a real comfort," he replied with a laugh, giving her a quick hug. "We'll get our sail one of these weekends, I promise."

Silently, with their arms about each other's waist, they walked in the firm, wet sand at the water's edge back toward Palmetto House.

After a restless night, Stephanie awoke Monday morning to a shadowy dawn. Her very first thought was that Benedict would be back sometime that day. Closing her eyes, she let herself drift and dream drowsily, happy in the anticipation of seeing him. Maybe they would swim tonight after rehearsal, and then as they walked along the beach, he would tell her all about his weekend. As pleas-

ant as the imagined scene was, though, something was
wrong. Filtering through her pretty dream came a vague
sense of uneasiness. She curled herself around her pil-
low, hugging it tightly against the undefined anxiety, and
listened to the measured ticking of her little clock. What
time was it, anyway? It was when she rolled over to look
that she discovered that Lynne's bed was empty—and
undisturbed. The little light Stephanie had left for her
roommate was still on.

In panic, she jumped up from her own bed and stood,
staring at Lynne's bed as if concentrating hard enough
would make her friend materialize. Friday afternoon
Lynne had gone with Jeff Hamilton, a childhood chum
and family friend, to spend the weekend as the guest of
his parents in their seaside villa in Hilton Head. She had
said that she would be back late Sunday evening. Obviously she had decided to spend another night, so there
was no need to imagine disasters, yet images of disasters
presented themselves by the dozens. Why hadn't Lynne
called to say she was going to stay another night?

Trying to distract her too active imagination, Stephanie walked over to the window and looked out on a deserted beach, a placid ocean and a pale turquoise sky. The
sun would be up any minute for the clouds already
glowed with a tender apricot color. Stephanie watched,
fascinated, as the apricot deepened to vibrant pinks and
corals. After a moment a sliver of brilliant orange appeared at the horizon. Then suddenly the sun, a pulsat-
ing, fiery sphere, was racing up the sky and turning the
ocean beneath it to gold.

"Please let Lynne be safe," she prayed, staring intently up through the bright morning.

After the morning workshops, Stephanie was enormously relieved to find Lynne, flaming red from sun-

burn, in the lobby waiting for her. As they headed for Valeriano's, Lynne told of how she and Jeff had gone sailing and had been hit by a storm. They were rescued after a night of bailing out gallons of water, and Jeff had to have the boat, which had struck something, towed back to the marina.

"What a terrifying experience!" Visions of what might have happened sent chills down Stephanie's spine.

"Yes, there were a couple of times when I thought we wouldn't make it," said Lynne with a little shiver.

"You must be exhausted. Why don't you skip class this afternoon and try to get some sleep?" suggested Stephanie.

"I'm fine, really. Besides, I wouldn't feel right skipping class."

After lunch, they went to their room. Stephanie saw it first. "Oh, look! There's something by our door."

"It looks like a florist's box. Oh, I bet it's from Jeff. How nice! He's already apologized a hundred times for last night. He's really very sweet."

Lynne cradled the box in her arms, and Stephanie saw that her friend was deeply touched. She also saw the quick change, like a light going out, when Lynne turned over the little white envelope and read the name. "Oh. This is for you." The disappointment in Lynne's face was also in her voice. She handed over the box.

"Who in the world?" Suddenly Stephanie was aware of the hard, rhythmic beating of her heart. Anticipation fluttered inside her like a bird with enormous wings. She turned the key in the lock three times the wrong way before she heard the customary little click.

With growing excitement, she slipped off the narrow, green ribbon and opened the box. Nestled in green florist's paper were five red rosebuds, tightly closed, shaped like giant teardrops.

"Open the card. See who they're from, or do you already know?"

Stephanie had known from the first moment but had not allowed herself to form the name until she read the confirmation on the little white card. It said, "Sorry about the weekend. Missed you. Benedict."

Lynne turned and, without a smile, went into the bathroom. Stephanie lifted the roses from their crisp nest as tenderly as if they were a newborn baby and looked at them a long time. Never before had she received roses from a man, and Benedict's gesture touched a soft place in her heart. They were so beautiful and so red.

That evening after dinner, Stephanie and Lynne, with *Carmen* books in hand, waited in the lobby of Palmetto House for Nick.

"I almost wish we didn't have rehearsal tonight," said Lynne. "I'm so tired I feel as if I could sleep for a week."

"It's probably going to be a hard evening's work. I'm dreading it a little bit, too," Stephanie admitted. This brief exchange, she reflected, was the first time either of them had mentioned *Carmen* to the other since Stephanie, struggling with a confusion of emotions, had congratulated Lynne on winning the coveted role.

Nick arrived, and the three of them walked to the Music Center. Stephanie became increasingly aware that she dreaded the evening more than a little bit. The closer they drew, the more pointed her disquietude became, until finally she knew that she absolutely could not go into that rehearsal room.

"You two go ahead. It's such a pretty evening, I think I'll sit here in the park a minute or two and just look at the ocean."

Both Lynne and Nick gave her puzzled looks but went on in. Stephanie sauntered over to the little seaside picnic area and sat down on one of the benches, but she didn't look at the sea. She looked at her hands suddenly clenched into fists in her lap.

"What am I going to do?" she asked aloud in a low, fierce voice. Then she crossed her knees and stacked her fists on them. She rested her forehead on her fists to think about it. She had sat motionless for several minutes when she heard someone approaching. The footsteps stopped just in front of her.

"Nick and Lynne said you came out here to watch the ocean." It was Benedict. He sat down and draped an arm across her back. "The ocean's that way." As Stephanie didn't move or speak, he continued, "What's the matter? Won't you tell me?"

"Nothing." Then silence.

"Stomachache?" Silence. "Headache?" Silence. "Any kind of ache?" Silence. "I'm running out of ideas, and I'd appreciate a little help with this. Can't you help a little?"

"Nothing's wrong. I just can't go in there."

"Sweetheart, why not?"

Then she lifted her head and, looking straight at him, said in a low, impassioned voice, "Because Lynne's in there. Lynne, Lynne, Lynne! Don't you understand?"

"I'm trying, but no, I don't. Why can't you go in there where Lynne is? You just walked over here with her. You sleep every night in a room with her. Do you see my difficulty?"

"Yes, but she doesn't sing *Carmen* in the streets or in bed at night."

"Oh. Oh, I see. Yes, yes, I do see." He was silent for a moment, then he continued. "You two seemed to be getting along so well, I thought you had worked all this out ages ago.''

"We decided to be professional about it.''

"What does that mean?''

"I haven't the foggiest. What we did was to ignore it completely, but just because you don't talk about it or don't behave spitefully doesn't mean it has gone away. I have been just miserable.''

"I had no idea, Stephanie. You've hidden it so well,'' said Benedict.

"And it isn't as if I don't like Lynne, I do. I adore her. She's my best friend, besides you. What am I going to do, Benedict?''

"Well, I don't see how you can sit out here all summer. Let's go in. Regardless of what you may be feeling now, I'd like you to have a look at Lynne tonight and tell me afterward what you think. Come on, give it a try.'' He stood up, pulling her along with him. "I've got to go. We're ready to begin.''

Stephanie's brain was a kaleidoscope of impressions and emotions, when later, during the break, she stepped outside into the soft, salty, night air. The bewitching rhythms of the rehearsal piano still throbbed in her veins, and in her mind's eye she could still see Lynne's Carmen. It was Lynne's Carmen that had shaken her to the very depths of her soul, that had brought her outside, desperately needing to be alone. She hadn't even begun to sort out her feelings when she heard someone behind her.

"I saw you sneak out,'' said Benedict. "What do you think now?''

"I think she's beyond anything,'' said Stephanie in a not-quite-steady voice.

She put her hand on his arm. "The thing that absolutely blows my mind is that while she is singing, I don't even see her blond hair and her peaches and cream skin—and those are the first things you always notice about her. She turns herself so completely into Carmen that there's not a shred of Lynne left visible. I don't see how she does it."

"I know. She takes my breath away, too," he said.

After a moment Stephanie admitted what her defensive pride so far this summer had refused to consider. "You know, Benedict, I honestly don't think I could do what I saw Lynne do tonight." Especially in your presence, she thought. She couldn't sing something as simple as "Three Blind Mice" for him.

From that night in early June when they had talked and made their truce, Benedict's words came back to her. "We chose Lynne not because you were so bad, but because she was so good." All right, maybe she could accept that now.

"I think I'm ready to face her," Stephanie said.

"Good for you." Benedict gave her a hug, and the two turned to go in.

They found her, as Stephanie expected they would, in the center of an animated group. All traces of fatigue had vanished from her face. Stephanie waited until she caught Lynne's eye. She sent her a smile that said, "I am so proud of you." At Lynne's responding smile, she rushed to her with outstretched arms. As they embraced, she said, "You were absolutely magnificent." She meant it with all her heart.

"Oh, Stephanie." Lynne's voice rang with relief and happiness; her eyes shimmered with tears. She caught Stephanie's hands in hers and pressed them hard.

When the break was over, Stephanie marvelled at how light and free she felt, but most of all, at how gently Benedict had encouraged her to face a hurdle with courage and an open mind.

Chapter Seven

Lynne, I don't think you ought to go dancing again to-night after rehearsal," said Stephanie, looking with concern at the dark circles under her roommate's eyes. They were dressing to go down to dinner. "You've been out every night this week until one or two o'clock. Jeff will understand."

Jeff had been in St. Cecelia since the accident, waiting for his sailboat to be repaired.

"He expects me to go and I hate not to since this is his last night here. But I must admit that I'm exhausted. I'll catch up on my sleep this weekend," she replied.

By the middle of the following week, Lynne was still listless and lethargic, and complained of a headache and a sore throat. Despite Stephanie's insistence that she stay in bed and rest, Lynne dragged herself with weary determination from workshop to rehearsal until Friday, when she awakened to discover painful, swollen glands in her neck. Feverish, she finally consented to remain in bed. Stephanie wanted to call a doctor. Lynne objected.

Late in the afternoon, Stephanie asked, "Would you like for me to call Benedict?"

"What for?"

"To tell him that you're not going to rehearsal," explained Stephanie.

"But I am going," Lynne replied. "I can't let him down."

"Lynne! Be sensible. Besides, there's Dierdre. That's what understudies are for."

"She hasn't learned the music yet. Benedict will have a fit."

"He's going to have one anyway if he sees you like this," said Stephanie. "I'd better call Dierdre, too, and tell her right now so she won't be taken by surprise tonight."

"No, Stephanie, not yet, please."

Though she wasn't able to eat a bite from her dinner tray, Lynne rose from her bed and began dressing for rehearsal. Stephanie felt her patient's forehead.

"You feel so hot, hotter than this morning. I wish you wouldn't do this. You're taking this business of the good little trouper way too far."

The short walk to the Music Center took forever. Lynne refused Stephanie's offer of a strong arm to lean upon and crept along at a snail's pace, stopping to rest every few steps. She seemed close to exhaustion. "This is madness, Lynne. Let's go back. You can barely stand."

"I am a little tired, but I think I can make it. I can't let them down."

All during the rehearsal of the first scene Stephanie hovered nervously over Lynne backstage, until it was time for the cigarette girls to sing their smoking song. Then the young soldiers asked, "Where is Carmencita?" and that was Carmen's cue to appear.

Stephanie, filled with anxiety, watched the wings. No Carmen. The piano stopped. Stephanie held her breath. Whispers flew. "Where's Lynne? Somebody call Lynne." Nick looked at Stephanie, his eyes full of alarm.

"Where is Carmen?" called Benedict, noticeably impatient. Stephanie, growing more tense by the minute, knew that this kind of inattention exasperated him. He had reminded them more than once that they were not school children putting on a play for the PTA. "Someone please call Carmen."

Stephanie, hardly breathing, her hand to her mouth, watched her roommate's approach. Lynne presented a peculiar Carmen. Her face was flushed; her eyes, glassy. She made her way through the crowd of young men, soldiers, and cigarette girls with a strange, shuffling step, her arms outstretched as if she were feeling her way through the dark. Steadying herself on an arm here, a back there, she finally reached center stage where she stood, swaying slightly. The entire company, frozen in its tracks, stared as if horror-stricken.

"Somebody help," screamed Stephanie, breaking ranks and rushing toward her.

A brief, wild desperation flared in Lynne's eyes, and then she crumpled in a heap of blue skirt and blond hair before Stephanie could reach her. Among the company, surprise turned to chaos. The rehearsal was in shambles.

The doctor's tentative diagnosis was a severe case of mononucleosis, but it would need to be confirmed by blood tests. He recommended that she go home immediately for complete rest and recovery under the care of her own doctor.

Saturday dawned bright and clear, a typical St. Cecelia day. Only this morning it seemed out of keeping with
the gloom in Stephanie's heart as she packed up Lynne's
things. The Kendricks would arrive just before noon to
take their daughter home. It seemed to Stephanie that the
telephone rang every ten minutes with calls from well-
wishers who were interested and concerned, but anxious
to keep their distance. She worried that she would not
have everything ready when Lynne's parents arrived, and
Lynne fretted that Stephanie shouldn't be doing that at
all and insisted that she would get up in a few minutes
and do it herself. Finally, though, everything was packed
and neatly lined up beside the door.

The Kendricks arrived, anxiety written large in their
gentle faces. They couldn't thank Stephanie enough for
her kindness to their daughter. When the trunk lid of the
car closed with a whump over the last piece of luggage,
the company of friends who had gathered to wish a pale
and hollow-eyed Lynne "Good health" and "Safe jour-
ney" burst spontaneously into an unpolished, but heart-
felt rendition of "She's a jolly good fellow." Stephanie,
watching with blurry eyes, was unable to sing. Hal Piersen, who would now have to find another tennis partner,
didn't sing, either.

Then Nick, waiting until Lynne was tenderly tucked
into the car, emerged from the group, bearing an armful
of long-stemmed red roses. He handed them through the
window to her and, as if on impulse, began singing the
flower song from the second act of *Carmen*. Lynne's finally getting her red roses, Stephanie thought, blinking
furiously and fumbling for a tissue. Nick ended his aria,
almost overcome. The automobile pulled out, and
Stephanie, burying her face in her hands, burst into sobs.
A pair of comforting arms went around her. It was Bene-

dict. He laid his cheek against her forehead and let her cry.

A few minutes later Stephanie, Nick and Benedict began walking in glum silence toward Valeriano's for lunch. Hal Piersen fell into step beside them, his hands in his pockets, his chin on his chest. He kicked aimlessly at the pine cones that happened to lie in his path. After a while he announced in a fierce, low voice, "I loved that girl."

"So did I," said Stephanie.

"And I," said Benedict.

"And I," added Nick.

For Stephanie, lunch was a difficult and gloomy affair, since the four of them, lost in private thoughts, hardly spoke. She looked around their little table at the three sad faces and realized that Lynne's departure had touched each of them in a profound way. A terrible sadness welled up in her heart for all of them, but especially for Benedict. A deep furrow was between his intense, dark eyes. The bottom had just dropped out of his opera-conducting debut. She touched his hand. "I'm so sorry," she said. "I know how you counted on her."

He looked at her briefly without smiling, then resumed his troubled gaze into space. Finally he said, "Well, it's Dierdre, I suppose." His voice was flat.

"Heaven help us." This came from Hal.

"Does it have to be?" asked Stephanie softly, hope suddenly stirring within her.

"Who else?"

"Stephanie," said Nick.

Hope jumped to its feet, eager and expectant.

"I wish she could," Benedict said, not even looking at her.

He said it too quickly; he didn't even consider it. He still didn't believe she could do it, and somehow his doubts ate away at the very foundations of her confidence in herself.

After lunch, on the way back to Palmetto House, Stephanie and Benedict took a slower pace and fell some distance behind Nick and Hal. "For the first time in my life," said Stephanie, "I'm not in the mood to work. Could I interest anyone in giving me a tennis lesson?" She offered him as bright a smile as she could manage.

"On any other day, you could, indeed. But I was just thinking that I ought to start right in with Dierdre and try to get her whipped into shape for rehearsal Monday night. I'm sorry, really, I am."

"Oh, that's all right. Of course, you should. I understand." It was hard not to show her disappointment. "Well, actually, I suppose I should go work, too, whether I'm in the mood or not."

A little while later Stephanie arrived at the practice studio and set her music, a bottle of Vitamin C and a large iced tea on the piano. She opened her music, took a vitamin with a sip of tea, and then swallowed again slowly, nervously alert for the first sign of a sore throat. After feeling her forehead, she explored the sides of her neck for swollen glands and was relieved when she found none. She began her warm-up. In a few minutes she stopped and listened. This very afternoon—a perfect afternoon for tennis—almost before the tears over Lynne's departure had dried, Benedict had replaced her with Dierdre. And they were somewhere in this building right now. Opening the door, she leaned out into the hall and listened but couldn't identify any sound as Dierdre's. A vivid image of the redhead danced before Stephanie's eyes. She gave the wooden chair in which she had been sitting a vigorous kick. It crashed harmlessly into the wall.

That evening at dinner, Dierdre and Benedict arrived together, each carrying music. He looked exhausted. She, in a pout, for once was not batting her extraordinary eyelashes. When Dierdre left, Benedict, bringing his coffee, came over to join Stephanie and Nick.

"How did it go?" she asked.

"We're back to square one," he replied. "First of all, Dierdre doesn't know the music, and she tries to divert attention from that by asking forty times an hour just exactly what do I want—perfectly silly questions—as if I were the world's most demanding conductor and she, the most long-suffering, put-upon singer."

"We're getting the picture," said Nick.

"That's not all," continued Benedict. "She apparently paid absolutely no attention to all those stage directions for Lynne that we worked out during the first rehearsals, so now we have to repeat all that for her benefit. The worst part of it is that she fights you the whole way. 'Why do you want me to do that? Why can't I stand here? I don't feel comfortable with that.'" In the tone and rhythm of his voice, Benedict had caught the essential Dierdre so clearly that Stephanie could imagine the scene as sharply as if she had been there.

"This has been a rough day for you," she said.

"To be absolutely fair about it, I have to admit that we caught Dierdre by surprise. Obviously she was not prepared for Lynne's sudden departure, but the thing that bothers the heck out of me is that she hasn't been working and keeping up. It's my fault, I guess, for not checking up on things better. I just assumed that we were all professional, responsible adults, and I was wrong."

"Poor Dierdre. Poor Benedict," she said, touching his arm briefly. "Poor everybody." And poor me.

Benedict took a long drink from his cup and said on the end of a heavy sigh, "We're going to have another go at it tonight, so I won't see you guys at the concert."

"Don't worry, Benedict. Dierdre's going to pull herself together and bring it off for you," said Stephanie, thinking how noble she sounded. As Nick rose to catch up with a friend who was about to leave the dining room, he turned to Stephanie and said, "See you in the lobby at eight-fifteen. After the concert, we'll do the town." He blew her a kiss and left.

Benedict frowned. "What does that mean?"

"Dear Nick," she murmured, watching him go.

"I said, 'What does that mean?'"

"What does what mean?" she asked, all innocence.

"What Nick just said and did? I've never seen him blow you kisses before. What do you two do when you do the town?"

"Do you want to come with us and find out?"

"Look, Stephanie, that's what I want to talk to you about."

"Nick? Whatever for?"

"No, not Nick. Dierdre. I may not be able to see you as much as I'd like for a while. It's going to take every minute of every day and night to get her ready. We don't have much time left. You understand, don't you? It's not the way I would like it, it's just the way things are."

"I know. I've got some work to do myself. Master Class is Thursday, and the matinee is coming up Sunday."

"Oh, that's right. What are you singing Thursday?"

"Dorabella's 'Implacable Desires.'"

"Good choice. I'm looking forward to it," said Benedict.

"Oh, no. I don't want you to come. You won't understand this, but I won't be able to sing if you come."

"Good heavens! Why?"

"I don't know. Just don't come." She looked him straight in the eyes to let him know she meant it.

"Are you serious?"

"Dead serious."

"Well, in that case..."

"Thank you. I knew you'd understand," she replied with a smile and secret sigh of relief.

In an attempt to fill the emptiness in her life made more unbearable by Benedict's long hours with Dierdre, Stephanie threw herself into her work with a grim, new determination. When the Humperdinck, the Strauss, and the Mozart selections held no more difficulties for her, she became obsessed with a compulsion to prove to herself that she could, indeed, sing the "Habañera"—and sing it properly. That she had sung it so badly in her audition was still a sore point for her. She finally arrived at the point of asking herself, why not sing it for Master Class and get some good, solid, professional criticism?

The great Metropolitan tenor, Giuliano Sebastiani, was to conduct the Master Class, and to receive the criticism of this gifted singer and genius of interpretation would be a once-in-a-lifetime experience for which any young artist would gladly give an arm and a leg. To have the Master point out the strengths and weaknesses of the performance and make suggestions for improvements was what Stephanie wanted for her "Habañera." If there were problems that could not be traced directly to Benedict's power to unsettle her, then she needed to know about them.

This was a new and daring idea. She would not have considered such a thing if Lynne were still there since Carmen had been Lynne's domain. To have done so would be presumptuous beyond words, but since Dierdre had not exactly laid claim to it yet—well, why not? The more she thought about it, the more reasonable and attractive it seemed. The only thing was, they were going to have printed programs, and it was probably too late to make the change. She had signed up for the Mozart.

On Thursday morning, while getting ready for Master Class, Stephanie decided she might as well go all the way. If she managed to get up the courage at the last minute to sing the "Habañera" instead of the Mozart, she should be dressed for it. She would fling fate the ultimate challenge by wearing her red and white dress and her red shoes, the outfit she had worn for the audition. Already she was nervous, and the class was still three hours away.

The appointed time finally arrived, and Stephanie walked into a room that was packed. A large number of townspeople, as well as all the Opera Fellows, waited in electric anticipation for the entrance of the beloved Metropolitan tenor. Enthusiastic applause and shrill whistles greeted Sebastiani's appearance. He smiled, arms outstretched to include them all, bowed several times, and finally blew kisses to them with gestures almost larger than life.

After Sebastiani said a few words about his great pleasure in being able to encourage young talent, the class began. Students sang, and the Master offered comments, all very constructive and supportive but right on target, thought Stephanie.

Her stomach had done flip-flops when she'd noticed on the program that Dierdre was scheduled to sing "Habañera" just before the morning intermission. She, herself, was listed as singing the Mozart in the next-to-last position before lunch break. She agonized about what to do. A dozen times she wiped her cold, clammy hands down the side of her skirt and told herself that she had better just stick to the Mozart.

When Dierdre stood to sing, Stephanie's heart squeezed itself into a tight little nut. But she had to admit that Dierdre handled her assignment with a nice touch. She had a beautiful voice and seemed at ease in front of the audience. When Sebastiani made several suggestions and then asked her to sing several parts over, Stephanie was surprised. What would Sebastiani say about her own "Habañera?" she wondered.

During the rest of the class, she tried, not very successfully, to relax and pay attention to the way her colleagues were singing and to what Sebastiani was saying to them. She found his criticisms as valuable as anything she had learned all summer. What wouldn't she give to be able to study with someone like him?

When her turn came, her heart immediately beat a rapid tattoo, and her knees went weak. Her heels echoed too loudly on the wooden floor as she walked toward the piano, and self-consciously she began to tiptoe. After she turned to face her audience, she gulped and then blurted out, "All of a sudden, I'm really nervous." She hadn't meant to say that. A burst of sympathetic laughter rippled around the room.

"Believe me, I understand. Just take a minute and relax," said the Master Singer, smiling.

What was she going to do? She desperately wanted the benefit of his criticism for her "Habañera," yet, to encroach upon Dierdre's territory and to profit in public from her mistakes seemed to Stephanie an ignoble thing to do. Quickly she scanned the assembly to assure her-

self that Benedict had kept his promise of staying away.
Then she lifted her chin, took a long, slow breath, and
signaled for her accompanist to begin. She closed her eyes
briefly, and when she opened them, the audience was
only a blur.

Halfway through the Mozart, Stephanie's knees still
felt weak, and she was still singing over a stomachful of
butterflies. She had expected her nervousness to subside
once she got into the music. That she had failed to relax
worried her a bit, for she was afraid the tension would
show in her voice. On the positive side, she had to admit
that she felt an exhilarating surge of power and energy
this morning.

When the last words had been sung, Stephanie waited
politely for the applause, but there was absolute silence.
In panic, she turned to look at Sebastiani, who was staring at her with an odd expression on his face. She had
failed again. Her mistake this time was spending so much
time on the "Habañera" when she should have been
working on the Mozart. She thought she had mastered
the Mozart, but obviously she had been overconfident.
Then, unsure of what to do next, she started back to her
chair in humiliation. When Benedict hears of this, I'll
just die, she thought.

Finally it broke—an explosion of applause. One by
one, two by two, she saw the audience stand until the entire room was on its feet, clapping wildly. In utter aston-
ishment, Stephanie put her hands to her face, turned her
back to the clamor and burst into tears.

When it was quiet again, the Master said, "What can
I say to you? You have won the approval of a very dis-
cerning audience. Justly, too, I might say. You were
marvelous. I liked especially the way you shaped the
phrases and colored the tone to reflect the emotional

content of the text. You've had some very good training, and it shows. You're very young yet, but that instrument of yours shows wonderful promise. Treasure your gift. Never force it or rush it. Let it bloom naturally. Don't be tempted to sing roles that you are not quite ready for. Good luck to you, Miss Morrison."

"Thank you. Oh, thank you very much," said Stephanie, incredulous and floating somewhere near the ceiling. "But, sir, I was hoping you would give me some pointers on how I could improve."

"Since you asked, I will. It is customary to acknowledge such gracious applause by bowing. Wasn't she splendid, ladies and gentlemen?"

The audience chuckled and then responded with another round of vigorous applause. Just as she was completing her bow, she saw Benedict standing in the hall just outside the doorway. He was beaming and clapping harder than anyone. She was too elated to be angry.

After the class was over, Sebastiani said to her, "Young lady, you have a wonderful future ahead of you."

Nick said, "Just what I thought."

Benedict asked, "Why didn't you sing like that for me?"

That afternoon on the way home from the practice studio, Stephanie stopped in a little shop in the square and bought a get well card for Lynne. At dinner and during the rehearsal that evening she passed the card around so all the members of the cast could sign it.

Benedict said, "I'm so glad you're doing this. I had thought of it, but I've been so tied up I've just not had a moment. I think it would be nice for us to send her some flowers, too, in a day or so. I'll try to remember to do it."

"I'll be glad to take care of it, Benedict. I know you're busy," said Stephanie.

"Thank you, Stephanie. What would I do without you?"

Later that night in her room, Stephanie wondered how he was doing without her. She was not very happy doing without him; she missed him terribly—the moonlight swims, the walks hand in hand on the beach, the parting kisses at her door. It seemed to her, as she sat at her desk, that life had lost a bit of its sparkle. In front of her lay a blank sheet of paper, a pen and Lynne's card now all covered with brief messages and signatures. It was growing late; she must get Lynne's letter written and go to bed. She was tired. Rehearsal had been exhausting.

All too soon, Sunday came. In the afternoon, the Opera Fellows not singing major roles in *Carmen* would present their matinee program entitled Introduction to the Opera.

At two-thirty in the afternoon Stephanie hurried to the St. Cecelia Theater in the Music Center, doing battle, as usual, with a case of pre-performance jitters. She loved the St. Cecelia Theater. Smaller than the concert hall, it was the perfect showcase, acoustically, for the Introduction, and the intimate setting gave her a comfortable rapport with the audience.

Stephanie knew before the last bow had been taken and the last of the applause had died away that she had sung well. To their credit, the whole ensemble had performed with all the refinement and polish they would have lavished upon a fully staged production. Backstage, flushed with the pleasure of their success, they were all talking too fast and laughing at the slightest provocation, when she noticed Benedict advancing toward her. She stopped mid-sentence, put her hands on her hips and tried to stare him down.

"Just what are you doing here? You promised, Benedict." They walked into the hall, out of earshot of the rest of the cast. "Besides, I thought you were working with Dierdre. How come you're not with her?"

He addressed an imaginary companion. "This woman really knows how to gladden the heart." To her he said, "My dog is happier to see me than you are."

"I'm happy to see you when you behave. I told you not to come. I thought you understood that you were not to hide in the curtains or under the rug or to eavesdrop from behind doors. You're right. I'm not happy to see you."

"Well, I'm happy to see you. Very happy. You look nice in that dress. It's a pretty color. You're probably going to say it's petunia, but it looks like crape myrtle to me." He smiled at her engagingly.

"What exactly are you doing here?"

"Well, what is it? Petunia or crape myrtle?"

"I asked you a question. What are you doing here?"

"To be absolutely precise about it, I've come to take you out to dinner. I thought you might like to celebrate after your successful debut in St. Cecelia Theater."

She glared at him in exasperation. "You're not supposed to know whether it was successful or not."

"St. Cecelia doesn't produce failures. Or at least it hasn't yet. But the thing that scares me, is that there is always a first time. Are you coming? Come on, let's go."

"I can't go like this." She looked down at the floor-length, bare-shouldered, hot-pink taffeta gown she was wearing.

"Certainly, you can. Please do. You look so—"

"Nice?" She gave him a teasing, side-long glance.

"That's just what I was going to say."

Stephanie pretended to be unaware of the stares and turning heads as she walked with Benedict through St. Cecelia Square.

"Everyone we pass thinks you're just about the prettiest thing he's ever seen," said Benedict.

"Speak for yourself," she replied with just a touch of sauciness.

At La Mirabelle, they touched wineglasses over pink linen, pink carnations, which adorned each table, and candle glow. It was barely six o'clock. An ornate, lazily turning fan aroused a fruity bouquet from the wine. She looked at Benedict and smiled. She thought she just might die of happiness.

"I heard that this afternoon's Introduction to the Opera went well."

"Oh? Good. I'm glad."

"That the audience was very responsive, especially to you."

"Yes."

"That all of you worked well as an ensemble. That's quite a tribute."

"Thank you."

"That you sang with ravishing beauty and astonishing clarity. That your voice has a lush, warm, golden quality like honey."

"Wonderful!" This was good talk.

"That you showed sophisticated musicianship, that your technique approaches perfection."

"Oh, excellent."

"That even in moments of tricky articulation you were right there, precisely on pitch and in tempo."

"I think all the things you have heard are perfectly true," she said, pleased to the center of her being that at last she had proved herself to him. She smiled at him impishly in acknowledgment of her cheekiness in her own behalf.

"I expected you to be humble and grateful to me for telling you all this."

"Where did you hear all these things? Who told you? Was it Nick? It sounds just like Nick."

"No one told me. I heard it all with my own ears. You were fantastic."

"Benedict, you promised." The heat in her voice warned that she was ready for war.

"Wait a minute, now, before you unseat me and trample me to death. I said you would not see me there. Did you?"

"No," she admitted. "Where were you?"

"I was not hiding in the curtains or under the rug. I was back in the sound studio. I even made a tape, so you can hear it yourself sometime if you want to."

"Oh, Benedict, was that fair?"

"All's fair in love and war."

Too quickly, she countered, "And which, pray tell, are we in?" Then, as she felt the warmth rising to her face, she could have bitten her tongue.

"Do you want an answer to that?" It was just like him to pursue it.

"I believe it was just a rhetorical question—for effect rather than for information."

"I see." He took a sip of wine, set his glass down, and reached across the table to set hers down, also. Taking her hands in his, he looked deeply into her eyes for a few moments, then said, "If this is war, then I'll be a soldier for life."

When they emerged from the perpetual twilight of La Mirabelle, the sky was just beginning to show pink. "Let's take a brief turn around the square," suggested

Benedict. "Then, as much as I'd like to spend the evening with you, I've got to work with Dierdre again tonight."

Disappointment welled up inside her and squeezed her former happiness thin. Would Dierdre never learn that music?

Having completed the stroll around the square, they stopped in front of the fountain. "Want to make a wish?" asked Benedict, drawing a handful of clinking coins from his pocket. He picked out two pennies.

"No. Keep your money. I've already wasted three cents in there this summer. It doesn't work."

Benedict laughed. "You must have wished for things that weren't good for you."

"They were very good for me."

"Try again, it's not too late. Here," he said, proffering the penny a second time. "I'm going to make a wish. Let's do it together. Give me your hand. Now, close your eyes and wish hard."

But she couldn't. It was too late to wish for the one thing she most passionately wanted—the role of Carmen.

Chapter Eight

On Wednesday, it was too hot to hurry and too hot not to. Though her lunch felt heavy in her stomach, Stephanie would have moved along at a faster clip, but Nick, huffing and puffing and mopping his face constantly with his handkerchief, insisted upon maintaining a snail's pace. The thermometer in front of the bank confirmed what Stephanie suspected—the temperature had soared to a hundred and six. As she and Nick plodded toward Palmetto House, she felt every one of those degrees.

Just as they were crossing the cool lobby with its little forest of growing green things, the clerk called out from behind the registration desk. "Miss Morrison, I have a message for you." He handed her a slip of pink paper.

"I wonder what this is all about," she said. "I'm to call a Ms. Corelli at an out-of-town number."

"Well," said Nick, pausing from his mopping up long enough to peer over her shoulder at the note, "you'll never know unless you find out. If it's good news, we'll celebrate. If it's bad, you can cry on my shoulder.''

"I hope I don't need to cry on your shoulder any more this summer. Anyway, I'll see you tonight at dinner, if not before," she said as the elevator stopped at her floor.

Upon reaching her room, she went straight to the telephone. Stephanie held her breath as Ms. Corelli identified herself as an executive assistant to the artistic director of a television program. Would Miss Morrison, Ms. Corelli wanted to know, be available in mid-December to sing with Giuliano Sebastiani at the Lincoln Center in New York City in a televised program to introduce talented young American opera singers?

"Would I what? Yes, I mean, uh, when did you say?" she asked foolishly, as if the date mattered. Of course, she would sing with him. She would move heaven and earth to do it, anytime, anywhere in the world. She could hardly think.

"You would need to be in New York the fifteenth, sixteenth and seventeenth, probably," Ms. Corelli replied. "But we'll be in touch with you again regarding the details."

"That's fine," said Stephanie, trying to keep her voice steady. "No problem."

Her hand trembled as she replaced the receiver. Stunned, she sat motionless on her bed, not daring to believe the unbelievable. Did what she think just happened really happen to her, to Stephanie Morrison? She looked again at the scrap of pink paper in her hand. Visible proof, it was now crumpled and damp.

Then a wild elation erupted inside her. She sprang from her bed and, half-laughing, half-crying, ran up the stairs two at a time to Nick's room.

After she told him, he insisted they celebrate. They went to Valeriano's and drank champagne. Doing so in the middle of the day seemed wonderfully impulsive, so deliciously decadent. "Oh, I love this, Nick. I'll remember this the rest of my life."

Her euphoria lasted all the way through chorus rehearsal. For the first time this summer, she didn't mind in the least that she was a mere cigarette girl in the opera. As she was leaving the rehearsal room, she glanced in Benedict's direction, as she did every day, and always, when their eyes met, they would exchange secret smiles that said something like, "You have the most adorable ears." Today her smile said, "If only you knew." His response was a raised eyebrow. For some reason that she didn't quite understand, she decided not to tell Benedict her good news. That Nick would tell him she was certain; she would like it that way.

Yielding to impulse en route to the practice studio, she stopped by to see her coach. When she told him, he said, "I'm not a bit surprised." He saluted her on the cheek with a noisy kiss, prickly with blond mustache. "This kind of thing doesn't happen every day. Come on; I'll buy you a glass of champagne. We'll celebrate." His pride in her shone in his eyes.

Not far from giggling, Stephanie submitted to a second trip to Valeriano's with sweetness and grace. Champagne was good for her.

Afterward, on her way to the practice studio, she wondered if Benedict knew yet. Maybe she should seek him out and tell him herself. Though she was impatient for him to know, she decided to give Nick a little more time. If by the dinner hour, Benedict hadn't come rushing to her, sweeping her up in his arms and covering her with a thousand congratulatory kisses, all the while telling her how wonderful she was, she'd have to tell him herself, even though it wouldn't be as much fun.

That decided, she settled down in front of the piano, opened her music, and stared at it. It swam before her eyes. Every time she caught the sound of footsteps approaching out in the corridor, she held her breath in tremulous anticipation, then sighed as they passed by. She wondered if, when Benedict finally found out, he would propose a glass of champagne to celebrate. Wouldn't that be funny, three glasses of champagne in one day after a whole lifetime of none at all? She laughed aloud and then wished that he would hurry up and find her.

Her impatience mounted as an hour and a half passed without incident. It was useless to stay any longer, but not five minutes after she arrived at her room, the telephone rang. It was Benedict, finally. She knew why he was calling.

"What's this I hear about you?"

"I don't know. What have you heard?" She hadn't intended to be coy.

"Why didn't you tell me, you little minx? Nick told me just a few minutes ago. I think this calls for a celebration. Meet me at Valeriano's in ten minutes and we'll have some champagne."

I knew it, I knew it, she thought, smiling to herself.

Her heart sang as she hurried to meet him. Unmindful of the heat, she could hardly wait. Champagne with Benedict wouldn't be simply champagne. There was something about him that imbued even the simplest experience with a shining vividness that sparkled in the memory long after. This would be the very best of the celebrations. But that was not all. She imagined his delight at her telling him that she would be in New York for three whole days in December. While they drank their champagne, they could plan a winter rendezvous. She smiled in anticipation and then at everyone she met.

She was the first to arrive and stood peering out the window watching for his approach. When he turned into the square, she could barely restrain herself from running to meet him, arms outstretched.

"Well, well, well," said Benedict as he joined her. "Congratulations." He gave her a little peck on the cheek. She looked at him, puzzled. She had expected more, even though they were in public.

"Aren't you pleased?" she asked.

"Oh, yes. Very."

"Were you surprised?"

"I guess so."

"Oh, my. I do wish you had said no."

"I'm not saying you don't deserve it. You do. I'm surprised in the sense that it's a rare thing to be singled out in this way, but not in the sense that I think he made a wrong choice. I think he made a wonderful choice. This summer, you've made dramatic improvements in your singing. You've blossomed like a rose, almost overnight. I wouldn't have believed it possible, if I hadn't heard you."

The little speech wasn't very festive; neither was Benedict. A vague anxiety rippled through Stephanie like a chill. Before she could identify its cause, the maître d' arrived to show them to a table. When Benedict ordered two glasses of champagne from the waiter who had twice served her similar orders, Stephanie suppressed a giggle at the look on the young man's face. She warned him with her eyes that he was not to say a word.

"To your success," said Benedict, raising his glass with its dancing bubbles. He smiled again, looking deeply into her eyes. It was a smile that obviously cost him some effort, and she knew all at once that he was exhausted. He looked as if he hadn't slept in days. His eyes, once all sparkle and dancing fires, were dull; his face, pale and haggard. An aching sympathy for him settled within her.

"Are you feeling all right, Benedict?"

"Oh, yes, fine. Why do you ask?"

"Well, you don't seem to be quite yourself today."

He cocked an eyebrow. "How so?"

"You look tired, and then there's this little frown—no it's a big frown—right here." She leaned toward him and touched his forehead. He caught her hand and kissed the tips of her fingers. "You're worried, aren't you?" she continued.

"No, no. As I said, I'm fine."

"If you want to talk about it, I'm here for you. I promise it won't go any further." She smiled, inviting confidences.

"Thanks, I know that, but I think I can handle it. I've got to." His voice was flat; his face, grim.

"Well, I wish I could do something to make it easier for you. I hate seeing you like this."

"You're very dear, Stephanie, but there's no point in involving you in my problems."

"But that's what friends are for." She reached across the table, caught both his hands in hers and looked into his eyes for a long, solemn moment. He leaned toward her over the tiny table and kissed her full on the mouth.

"More than friend," he said.

Stephanie's heart burned. *More than friend.* The statement thrilled her at the same time that it alarmed her. Why should she be alarmed? Was it possible for two ambitious, career-oriented musicians to be more than friends and yet remain just friends? Was there a special dispensation of grace for those who loved music with a sacrificial devotion, for people like her and Benedict?

She looked across the table at the extraordinary face whose clean planes and strong lines were written indelibly in her heart. His eyes had come to life and now, inscrutable and serious, they regarded her with an unsettling intensity. Could he be reading her thoughts? Was he wondering, as she was, if the two of them were destined to break each other's heart come September? She could bear the moment no longer. Without smiling, she touched a finger to her lips, then reached across the table to touch his.

"This is your celebration," he said. "Let's talk about you."

"There isn't much to say. Nick's already told you."

"Why didn't you tell me?"

"I don't know, really. Maybe our distant past."

"After all this time? That's water under the bridge, Stephanie. Are you still holding that against me?"

"I don't know. I said, maybe. Maybe I didn't want to flaunt my victory in your face as if to say, 'See there, I told you so. Look what a terrible mistake you made.' Does that make sense?"

"I'm surprised. I had no idea you were still agonizing over this."

"Benedict, let me say this and then I won't mention it again—ever." She paused to draw a deep breath. "I have wanted Carmen more than I've ever wanted anything in my whole life—everyday, all day long, this entire summer."

"You break my heart. You still think I could have given it to you, but didn't."

"No, no. I understand why I didn't get it. It's all right, now. Really it is. In fact, I think, in the eternal scheme of things, it was probably good for me not to get it."

"Why, Stephanie?"

"Because nothing in my past had prepared me for failure. I didn't know how to cope with it, but I know now that you have to find ways of making peace with yourself so that it doesn't destroy you. It was a hard, but necessary lesson. I only wish it hadn't happened with you. I wish you might have been spared all the pain of my having to learn it." Suddenly she choked over the words, and tears smarted in her eyes. She gave a helpless little shrug and blinked furiously. "Sorry."

His eyes took on an odd intensity as he studied her face. He bent toward her. "Stephanie, I wonder... well, it occurred to me that since Dierdre—" His inspiration was apparently a fleeting one, for he halted abruptly and, shifting his gaze, bent all his attention to contemplating the slow rise of the few remaining bubbles in his dying champagne.

"You wondered what, Benedict?" She reached across the table to touch his hand, to draw him back to her. Was he finally going to offer her the role of Carmen?

"Never mind," he said. "It wasn't a good idea." When he looked at her again, his eyes showed only a dull fatigue. He drained his glass and set it down with an air of finality. They walked back to the inn without speaking.

As much as she loved the opera, Stephanie grew to dread the evening rehearsals, which now progressed in fits and starts. Dierdre pulled a variety of show-stoppers from an inexhaustible repertory of complaints. Benedict was harassing her, the rehearsal piano was too soft, the tempo was too slow, Nick was upstaging her, Benedict was a slave driver, she wasn't having a good time, and on and on.

The company grew more impatient daily, and understandably more intolerant of Dierdre's caprices, while Stephanie watched with aching heart Benedict's valiant attempt to control his temper despite the provocations and his own increasing frustrations.

The most serious problem, however, was Dierdre's failure to do her homework. She still had not learned all the music. Rumor said that Benedict was desperate to make her learn it, and, to that end, they worked all day and straight on through the night. Stephanie longed for an invitation from Benedict to go swimming again, and at the end of each rehearsal, she waited—in vain. Wincing, she watched Dierdre and Benedict disappear every night into his office. She would not name the tide of misery that washed over her, but she was sure its color was green.

One evening in early August, the tension exploded. Dierdre, having worked herself into a frenzy, suddenly jerked off one of her heavy wooden clogs, hurled it with all her might straight at Benedict, and ran from the room, shouting a barrage of profanity, which crackled in the charged air like firecrackers.

The clog hit him in the temple beside his left eye. His hand flew to his head. He staggered and then bent double. Stephanie, frozen with horror at first, somehow made her feet move, rushed to his side and finally succeeded in persuading him to sit down. Blood drizzled down his cheek and made purplish blotches on his pale blue shirt.

"Ice," she commanded. "Somebody get ice."

Shock and confusion reduced the company to chaos. The singers milled around, talking excitedly, not knowing what to do until Phillip dismissed them. Stephanie accompanied Benedict to his room where, with shaking hands, she tenderly washed the blood from his face and applied three Band-Aids in a row in lieu of a proper bandage. "How do you feel?"

"Not too bad, it's nothing. I should have stayed. We need the rehearsal time."

"Rehearsing tonight would be a total waste of time, Benedict. Nobody's in the mood now. You just relax for a change." She led him to his bed.

"Do you realize that opening night is three and a half weeks away and we have no Carmen. We have no opera. What in heaven's name am I going to do?"

"You can't do a thing tonight," she said, fluffing his pillows and piling them up for him to lean against. After pulling off his well-polished loafers, she said, "You just take it easy, and I'll put on some water for a nice cup of tea. While it's heating, I'll pop down the hall and get some more ice. You should put ice on that every half hour or so and maybe you won't get a huge bump."

"I'm not incapacitated. I'll put on the water." He started to get up. "Ooooo. Oh, my gosh." He moaned and sat back down, his hand to his head, his face suddenly contorted.

"Stay where you are. I'll get you some aspirin."

"I'm perfectly fine. I don't need you to nurse me. I can get my own aspirin."

"Lie back down on those pillows this instant." She handed him a cup of water and two little white pills. "Now, down the hatch with those aspirin."

When she returned with the ice, the water in the electric kettle was boiling. After she brewed them each a cup of Earl Grey, she pulled up a chair and sat down. With tender solicitude, she watched him as he sipped. How homey and cozy it seemed.

He looked over at her then and smiled a simple smile that seemed to say, "Well, here we are, just the two of us." It flew straight as an arrow to the softest place in her heart and found a home there.

She looked back at him with a smile that said, "One of your socks is on wrong side out, but it's all right. It's just the two of us. I understand."

He looked terrible. She'd never seen him look worse. Maybe that was why, all of a sudden, she knew that she loved him. She laughed softly.

"What is it?" he asked.

"Oh, nothing. Nothing, really."

"You laughed."

"I know. It's nothing. You have a sock on wrong side out." Other than that, my darling, nothing at all, except that I love you. Hopelessly. With all my heart. And what is going to become of us, I don't know.

On the following Sunday afternoon, the palms cast long shadows across the parking lot as Stephanie handed Benedict her car key.

"What is this thing?" he demanded, frowning with his one good eyebrow. He was still sporting a huge purple knot on his head.

"That is a Spam key. It works. You'll see."

He glared at her. "I don't like this at all. Why don't you get a replacement? It's crazy to drive around with a Spam key. What if something were to happen?"

"What could happen? That works perfectly well, except for unlocking doors, so I don't lock them. I'll drive if you don't like my key."

In answer, he clicked his seat belt and ground the ignition. The Volkswagen coughed and sputtered. They were on their way to the mainland for dinner in an old plantation house that had been restored and was now a popular restaurant. They drove along a back country road through a bland, low-country landscape of pines and scrub oaks. The road was narrow, crumbling at the edges. Occasionally it went past marshes where cypresses festooned with grizzled Spanish moss stood knee-deep in ancient black water.

Eventually they turned into a narrow lane paved with crushed oyster shells and at the end of a double row of gigantic live oaks, obviously hundreds of years old, the mansion came into view. It had once been the center of a rice and indigo plantation.

After nosing the car into a parking place, they immediately set out for a stroll through the gardens. They came upon a secluded green space enclosed by hedges. Like a room, it was furnished with a pair of benches and a statue of a chubby child feeding pigeons. Benedict led Stephanie to one of the benches and placed on her lap a parcel that he had stashed in her car and then retrieved upon their arrival.

"This is for you. I hope you like it."

It took forever to get the brown paper wrapping off.

"Oh, a music box! How gorgeous! I love it."

"Let me wind it for you."

The music box began its metallic, deadly-in-earnest rendition while the little female figure on top turned in a slow dance.

"The 'Habañera!' Oh, it's Carmen," she said, gazing at the rotating form.

"Your song. Or, maybe, our song." He looked at her oddly, almost wistfully.

"It's just beautiful. Thank you ever so much."

After exclaiming over every remaining vista in the garden, they returned to the house where they ordered dinner. They had just pronounced the veal marsala marvelous when all of a sudden the string quartet left its station in front of the fireplace and came to stand beside their table. At a slight backward tilt of the head from the first violinist, they launched into the "Habañera," playing it in an oddly provocative freestyle rhythm. Stephanie was both delighted and embarrassed.

"How did they know to do that?" she asked.

"They took one look at us and knew right off the bat that the 'Habañera' was our song."

"That's crazy." How did the "Habañera" suddenly get to be their song? She began putting one and one together and inevitably came up with two. Could it be that he was setting the stage for something special? She searched his face for a clue and found him looking at her again with that same strange intensity. Was he going to propose? A thrill shot through her. What was she going to say? What about their careers? It would never work, of course, with her in Chicago and him in New York. Also, she was too young. She had met him too soon. On the other hand, she loved him dearly; and she couldn't bear the thought of losing him. What to do? She was so excited she couldn't think. She reached across the table and rested her hand lightly on his.

"The 'Habañera' was lovely." All atwitter, she looked at him expectantly. At this moment she didn't understand herself at all, but the moment passed, and by the time they finished their cappuccinos, she had decided that her intuition was wrong. She was both relieved and disappointed.

After dinner, they strolled again into the garden and sat on a stone bench where they could see the river, apricot now in the final flush of sunset. Benedict reached into his pocket. Oh, here it comes. Stephanie's heart took flight again. First he would tell her that he loved her. Then he would take her hand and press it to his lips, and then . . . She waited.

He pulled out a piece of folded paper. Handing it to her, he said, "Look at that."

Surprised and puzzled, she opened it and gave it a cursory glance. "It's just a bunch of names," she said, deflated.

"Look again."

"Oh." It was a cry of anguish. The Opera Fellows were petitioning Benedict to ask her to take the role of Carmen and save their production. She refolded the paper and handed it back to him. "No," she said, not looking at him.

"No?"

"Yes, no. Why didn't you ask me in St. Cecelia? You make me feel like an absolute monster saying no after all this. But no, anyway." She crossed her arms in front and held onto herself.

"I thought you'd want to. You said you'd wanted it all summer."

"Three weeks before opening night? There isn't time for me to do what the music deserves, or what I require of myself. Why don't you get someone who has sung the part to come in?"

"I tried all weekend. Everyone's on vacation, or they all have commitments already." He was silent for a moment, then said, "So that's that. You won't change your mind?"

She shook her head, looking him squarely in the eyes. His face was noncommittal. This was puzzling to her. Why was he not pulling his hair?

Since their business meeting was obviously over, they rose and meandered down first one path and then another, looking at nothing in particular, saying nothing. Stephanie noticed that in one edge of the sky black clouds were beginning to form. There would be rain, as usual, later that night.

It was growing dark when they ended their not-quite-companionable garden walk and wandered down to the river and out onto the pier. Around the shoreline lights twinkled like fallen stars tangled in the dark woods. Out over the river the night sky was incandescent with the promise of a moon. Shimmering and shifting in the growing light, the quicksilver water seemed alive, rising and falling, lapping against the pilings. The pier swayed slightly.

Other couples sauntered onto the pier, their arms around each other. A young man began playing a lovesick tune on his guitar. A breeze stirred, ballooning Stephanie's skirt and swirling her hair across her face. She looked up at Benedict and longed for him to say the word that would make everything all right between them again.

The opalescent moon emerged, casting a silvery glow on everything. The women turned in their lovers' arms, faces uplifted to receive kisses. Stephanie, feeling confused and betrayed, turned away from Benedict and, again folding her arms across her chest, stared out at the water.

"We're going to have to cancel the opera," Benedict finally said from behind her, as if their early conversation had continued all this time uninterrupted. "Don't you care?"

"That's too bad," she replied, not turning her face to him. "Can't you at least present a program of vocal and orchestral selections?"

"That's not an opera."

It grew darker as the clouds obscured the moon. "It's going to rain. We'd better go," he said.

Stephanie, relieved that the evening was ending at last, started for the car, only to realize that an hour's drive cooped up in that Volkswagen lay ahead of them.

By the time they reached the parking lot, lightning flared and thunder rumbled, belated and distant. Before they reached the end of the oyster shell lane, the rain began. At first huge drops smashed themselves flat on the windshield, then a deluge surrounded them with a roaring, opaque curtain of dead gray, impenetrable by headlights.

Benedict hunched over the steering wheel, peering intently at the watery world, driving slowly as if feeling his way along. In a frenzy, the windshield wipers went slap-slap, slap-slap. Stephanie held her breath every time the sky went lurid with lightning. Thunder now cracked right over their heads. The wind, like a huge wet towel, smacked the rain against the car, which rocked under the blow.

As they crept along, an eerie sound, like the scraping of metal on glass, added a ghostly accompaniment to the noise of the engine and the roar of the storm. The car slowed to a crawl as a heavy sheet of water blotted out Benedict's view entirely. Carefully, he brought the car to a stop on the shoulder. The windshield wiper blade had flung itself off.

"This should be over in a few minutes. When it slackens, I'll try to find the blade and we'll be on our way," said Benedict.

For what seemed like hours, they waited while the rain drummed on their roof. When the storm finally began to abate, Benedict decided to back up the car and illuminate the area with the headlights. But the Volkswagen was through for the night. Though Benedict ground the ignition for a long time, there was no response. Fearing the carburetor was flooded, he waited a bit and then tried again. After another wait, during which Stephanie knew he was becoming more frustrated and impatient, he attacked again. Immediately she heard a small sound, as of metal snapping, and then a string of words under the breath that she had not heard from him since that rainy Friday of the audition when she had dropped her tote bag.

"This stupid Spam key's broken off in the switch. We've had it now. We should never have been out driving around with this thing in the first place. I knew something like this would happen. How do you suppose we're going to get home now?"

"We'll wait right here for someone to come by, or we could go to someone's house and use the telephone," she suggested.

"How many cars have you seen come by here? Look around. How many welcoming lights do you see shining from windows? None. Nobody lives in this forsaken swamp."

"What do you suggest that we do, then?" she asked.

"We'll wait right here for someone to come by."

They sat in silence for a long time. Finally Stephanie said, "I'm sorry, Benedict, truly I am. About everything. This has been a really rotten evening for you. On top of everything else."

"It wasn't your fault."

"I feel responsible for part of it, at least."

She sat quietly for a long time; it seemed like about two weeks. The dark was unrelieved and ominous with unseen presences. She grew restless and bored. Finally she reached for the music box and wound it up. From her lap came the mechanical tinkle of "Habañera." When it ended, she played it again, and as it wound down the second time, Benedict said, "We are in a crisis, Stephanie. Does that make any difference to you?"

"It's not so bad. Someone will come by soon."

"I mean the opera company. We have patrons who have bought tickets, and as of now, there is no opera. The company has worked hard all summer, and there will be nothing to show for it. This may very well be the end of the St. Cecelia summer workshops, because the sponsors will think they are wasting their money. It will certainly mean that my opera conducting career will take a nosedive, but that is not the most important of the possible disasters. I'm thinking about the company and the patrons, Stephanie."

"Are you trying to make me feel guilty? Well, you've certainly succeeded. I feel miserable, but I don't see why all these disasters are, all of a sudden, my sole responsibility. It isn't fair."

"You're the one person right now who could prevent them."

"In three weeks? I'm not a miracle worker."

"Your coach said you're a quick study."

"Even quick studies can't do the impossible. I don't want to be another Dierdre. Besides, you know as well as I that no one can sing under that much stress."

"I'll help you, Stephanie. You know I'll do everything in my power to make it easy for you."

"I can't sing for you. Remember?"

"Horsefeathers!"

"I can't do it, Benedict. You're asking the impossible."

Again they fell into an uncomfortable silence, which grew more unbearable by the minute. The little car was too small for two people who couldn't talk to each other anymore. Frustrated and unhappy, Stephanie got out, picked her way in the dark through the wet grass around the car to the pavement. In absolute darkness, she paced short distances up and down the road, while all around her the air was heavy with the smell of wet pine and the rain-drenched earth.

When she had been walking for a while, he called to her from the car, "The company is one hundred percent behind you, Stephanie. They have absolute faith in you. Doesn't that make any difference to you?"

"Yes," she called back to the faceless voice in the dark. "It breaks my heart."

"Well?"

"I don't want to get their hopes up and then have the whole thing crash around their ears."

"They really want you."

Miserable, she resumed her walking. After a long time she crept back into the car. Benedict did not acknowledge her return.

Finally the sky began to lighten and gradually the absolute dark softened to a shadowy duskiness. As the light increased, she saw that they had spent the night in the middle of a forest, broken only by the road they were on. They must have taken a wrong turn in the storm. She didn't remember driving past any of this yesterday.

She turned to look at Benedict and found him looking at her. "What am I going to tell the company when we get back?"

"I expect you can think of something," she snapped. She couldn't stand this any longer. "All you can talk about is doing it for the company." She turned away quickly to hide the sudden tears that smarted in her eyes. "The truth is—" She choked over the sobs she could not control. "The truth is . . . you don't want me. You never have. Not from the very beginning. You don't think I can do it. In spite of the company, you don't want me. That's why I can't do it. So stop asking me."

"Don't cry, Stephanie. Look, sweetheart, I never meant for this to upset you." Anguish was in his voice. He put his arm across her shoulder, but she shrugged it off.

"All right, then. I don't want you." He was obviously reluctant, peeved even, to have to admit it.

She jerked her head around to stare at him, tears standing in her eyes, the sobbing shocked out of existence.

"You are perfectly right. I don't want you, and I'll tell you why. I want to spare you. To pull this thing off now would be an almost super-human task, and I don't want you to have to go through it. It would mean unrelenting work day and night from now until opening night. By then you would be worn to a frazzle, I'd be out of my mind, and we'd hate each other. I just don't want that to happen to us. But I had to ask you, don't you see, for the company.

"Besides, I really thought that you wanted it, but for some perverse reason, you needed me to beg you to take it. On the other hand, regardless of my personal feelings, I am still responsible for coming up with an opera, polished and ready to go on opening night. I feel that responsibility very strongly, so that even though I don't

want you to do it, I wish you would. Does all of this make
any sense to you?"

"Yes, I guess so."

"Will you do it then?"

"A truck! A truck! Oh, Benedict, a truck!" Stephanie was beside herself with relief.

Benedict tumbled out of the car even though the truck
appeared to be half a mile away. As it approached, he
signaled for it to stop. It was piled high with spiny tree
roots. When Benedict finished the tale of their plight, the
driver turned his head and with practiced lips sent an
amber stream arcing in the early sunlight to splat on the
pavement.

"Guv'nor," he said, blinking his watery blue eyes,
"they ain't nuttin' on this here road but the county dump.
Soon's I dump my load, I'm goin' back out to the main
road. I'll carry y'all that far. They's a feller in the gas
station what'll fix you up. Now, y'all set tight for mebbe
thirty minutes, and I'll be back, ya hear."

True to his word, he was back in half an hour, and
Stephanie and Benedict took their very first ride in a
dump truck, followed by a return trip in a tow truck.

The "feller" from the gas station fitted himself into the
Volkswagen and began work. "In my bidness, you hear
some strange thangs, but I declare if I ever heard tell of
driving a car with a Spam key," he said. "Now, this
here's gonna be a mean little bugger to get out of there."
But get it out he finally did. After towing them to the gas
station, he consulted an enormous book filled with columns of numbers, then made a key. And they were on
their way.

Chapter Nine

Chin in hand, Stephanie sat staring at the dull, flat landscape reeling past her window. She and Benedict had not spoken for at least a quarter of an hour. Not even the noisy chugging of the Volkswagen's engine could drown out the maelstrom of conflicting voices in her head. They questioned, accused and confronted her.

Benedict was desperate or he never would have asked you to take Carmen. You were his last resort, you know.

Being third choice hurts your pride. That's why you won't take it.

Not wanting to begin your career with a bad performance is just an excuse.

Which is worse, for you to have a bad performance or for the company to have no opera at all?

Do you think St. Cecelia exists for the sole purpose of making you a star?

That question was a jab in the ribs.

The voice continued. Aren't you letting the company down? Would Lynne have let the company down?

The answer, of course, was Lynne would never have let the company down. She would have sung with her dying breath. But that's the way Lynne was—totally unselfish, the very model of the good little trouper.

You're afraid of being a failure in Benedict's eyes? What do you think he's thinking about you right now?

Stephanie let out a sigh of exasperation and moved restlessly in her seat. What *was* Benedict thinking? She stole a glance at him out of the corner of her eye. His face had that gray look of defeat. Guilt did its work in her.

"I feel terrible." She blurted it out like an old woman's complaint.

He looked at her but said nothing. Several miles down the road, he swung onto an exit and nosed into a parking place beside a restaurant.

"Shall we get a bite to eat here? I'm not quite up to breakfast with the cast this morning," he said.

Guilt jabbed her again. It was in her power to save him, and she had refused. How would he tell them? She said only, "I'm not, either. I wish we didn't have to go back."

While they ate their scrambled eggs, Benedict said, "It's going to be a hot day." They had seconds on coffee and resumed their drive in silence.

Her conscience took up its argument again. You are supposed to be in love with him. Doesn't love mean anything more to you than a few thrilling kisses and a head full of romantic reveries? If you really love someone, aren't you willing to go the extra mile, to risk your neck, to attempt the impossible for him?

She looked at him. Did she love him that much?

Too soon they were at Palmetto House, and the Volkswagen shuddered to a halt. Benedict opened the door on his side but didn't get out. When she made a move to leave, he caught her hand and said, "Wait, I have something to say."

"The answer is still no, Benedict," but she said it almost apologetically. She loved him very much, but things that were impossible too often turned out to be imperfect when attempted. She couldn't stand turning in a performance that was less than perfect.

He responded with a look of aggrieved patience and cleared his throat. "This has been a bad experience for both of us, but I don't want you to feel guilty." His voice was flat with resignation; his face, haggard. "As for the opera, Stephanie, if you honestly feel that you've made the right decision, then I must respect it. If you are convinced you can't do it, then you probably can't. You know better than anyone else whether you can or can't."

"But I can, Benedict," she said, bristling slightly. "I mean, I could if I had more time. There just isn't time enough."

"And it's your career," he continued. "It would be madness for you to jeopardize it by trying something that seems destined to fail."

"Every singer accepting a new role takes a risk, Benedict," she said, irritated by his plodding attempt to be noble.

As if she hadn't spoken, his flat voice went on. "You see, when I asked you to take the role, I wasn't looking at it from your point of view. I was selfishly thinking about my own responsibility to produce an opera, but I know now that I can't sacrifice you to save my own face."

"I can't think of anyone who would consider singing *Carmen* a sacrifice," she said, and that was as close as she could come to offering herself as a sacrifice.

"But to learn it all in three weeks would mean giving up everything else," said Benedict.

"But it would be for just three weeks, and then it would all be over. Anyone crazy enough to accept the challenge could certainly hold out for three weeks." Was she that crazy? How much did she love him?

He continued as if determined to pursue his train of thought. "What I'd better do is just cancel the whole thing." His voice was heavy with despair. Her heart ached for him.

"What about the patrons?" she asked. He had been concerned about them earlier.

"Exchange the tickets or refund the money. A nuisance, but what else?"

"What about us? All the work we've put into it? Hours of rehearsal."

"Down the drain."

"And the sets, the props and the costumes? Since the only thing missing is a Carmen, it seems a shame to cancel."

"That's what I thought at first. What do you suggest?"

"Don't cancel." She looked him steadfastly in the eyes, promising him everything. She would attempt the impossible.

"I've already made up my mind. It's finished, Stephanie, there's no use beating a dead horse."

"It's a dark horse, not dead."

Frowning, he shot her a puzzled look. Then he said, as if it were the final word, "It would be too hard on you. I don't want to put you through it."

"I've done hard things before. Let's do it."

"It's no good, Stephanie. I'll tell the cast tonight."

"Well, at least, you'd have something for opening night. Let's do it. Do reconsider."

"It's not fair to you. You've worked hard on your assignments and given your performance. Enough's enough."

"I thrive on work. I can do it. With one hand behind me, for pete's sake. Say yes."

A light was beginning to shine in his eyes. "Are you sure? I don't want you to be unhappy."

"I'm sure." She turned to smile at him. "Oh, no, wait. I can't sing for you, remember?"

"Yes, I remember, that's why I didn't choose you in the first place. However, let's worry about that tomorrow."

As they walked toward the Music Center in the clear, bright morning air, she was suddenly overwhelmed by the foolhardiness of her decision to attempt the impossible. She had allowed sentimental notions about love to override reason. There would be no magic; not even gypsy music could bring about a miracle.

In the unquiet silence of her misgivings, she stopped still in her tracks. A heavy yoke seemed to settle on her shoulders. "I can't do it," she said, and her eyes implored him to release her.

He gave her a long, searching look. Then, without saying a word, he put his arm around her, and they resumed their walk.

When they reached his office Benedict said, "We'll concentrate on Act One today." He handed her the by-now dog-eared copy of the *Carmen* book.

"We, Benedict? Look, I think I could work more efficiently alone. At first, I mean."

"I know what you're thinking, and it won't work. You might as well get used to me right from the start." He kept his voice steady and quiet.

"You're going to make problems for me, and I don't need problems on top of everything else." In contrast to his, her voice rose in panic despite her effort to match his control.

"Well, we'll see what kinds of problems they are this morning."

"Benedict, seriously, I'd rather work alone."

"I know, Stephanie, but be reasonable. We don't have time now to stage a battle for supremacy. We'll work together this morning."

"If you're going to be that way, we can't work together. Because working together doesn't work that way."

Stephanie laid the book on Benedict's desk and sat down heavily in a gray metal chair, letting her hands drop between her knees. Benedict's face blanched.

In the end, they went to the rehearsal room together. "Shall we begin with a little warm-up?" he asked, sitting down at the piano. "Now, just relax. I'm not going to bite you. I'll even sing along with you."

She sang cautiously, keeping her voice soft, hiding it under his.

"How long does it take you to warm up? Can't you open up a little now?"

"I'll try," she said, but she was afraid to let go.

Later, even though he suggested that they go on to *Carmen*, she knew that he was not satisfied. "Take it easy until you feel more relaxed." She also knew that, try as she might, she would never be relaxed.

First they tackled the entire "Habañera" scene. Benedict played the piano and sang the parts of the cigarette

girls, the young men and the soldiers. When they finished, he looked at her oddly and said, "Shall we run that
again? Now, this time, forget that I am Benedict Delman. From now on, I'm Don José and you are a gypsy
peasant—hot-blooded, earthy, sensual, uninhibited.
Think about the words and warm up your voice to match
the words. Do what your instincts prompt you to do.
Okay?"

That was part of her problem. If she thought about the
words and followed her instinct, she would lay bare her
own soul and expose to him this tender fledgling love of
hers that was doomed anyway, but too new and precious
to be stared at, then rejected. She hadn't meant to fall in
love, but like a gypsy, it had stolen into where it had no
business being, in spite of her stout protestations that she
was going to be a career woman. That was problem
enough, and there was no point in compounding the
problem by allowing Benedict to know the affairs of her
heart.

Although he had said he wanted the usual things life
had to offer, he had also made it clear that right now he
was too busy with his career to think of marriage. What
a nuisance it would be for him to discover that she was
madly in love with him. He would feel trapped, and his
first impulse would be to disentangle himself. Disentan-
glement, of course, was the same thing as rejection. The
very idea brought a sharp stab of pain to her heart just
where that intruder, love, had burrowed in.

As for following her instincts in singing Carmen, she
was torn, because she had two opposing impulses. One
urged her to free her emotions and save Carmen; the
other warned her to hide them and keep Benedict.

After they had sung "Habañera" the second time, he said, "You must feel it before we can feel it, you know. Warm up the sound, now. Remember who you are."

She sang again and watched the effect in his face. Obviously he didn't know how to deal with her. She felt sorry for him and sorrier for herself. She knew she was singing with the thin, colorless voice of a seventeen-year-old.

"Passion, Stephanie, passion. This is not Mozart."

About mid-morning when they took a break, Benedict asked, "What's the problem, Stephanie?"

"It isn't anything that I can explain to you."

"How can I help you?"

"I don't think you can." She couldn't look at him.

"That's no answer," he said, almost angrily.

"Well, being cross is certainly not going to help." She knew he couldn't stand being stymied. "Don't you think we should cancel? Seriously? We both know now it isn't going to work."

She thought for a moment that he was going to agree, but he said, "Not yet. It'll come, Stephanie. It'll come if we keep working."

But it hadn't come when they stopped for lunch. They walked in silence to Valeriano's; he, looking perplexed and defeated, and she, feeling guilty for making him so.

During the afternoon they worked with Phillip and the other principals so that Stephanie could learn entrances, exits and other stage business. Standing rather awkwardly in the center of attention and finding new inhibitions in herself where there had been none, she gave an apologetic laugh and said, "I'm not very good at this. If you'll just tell me how many steps to take and which arm to raise, I'll do it."

Though Phillip showed her innumerable times just what he wanted, she knew her actions were lifeless, bloodless mimicry, nothing more.

"Carmen's not a nun, Stephanie," he said with some exasperation.

"I know. She's an earthy, sexy, gypsy peasant, which I'm not."

"Use your imagination. You know about being a woman. You know about men and flirting and being sexy." He looked at her for a moment, then added, "Or at least you've seen it in the movies."

Before long Phillip's face wore the same look of perplexity and worn patience that she had seen on Benedict's. Later she saw him turn to Benedict. As their eyes met, she read the message as clearly as if it had been flashed on a screen: this is hopeless. What are we going to do? But worst of all, she saw in Nick's eyes a look of blank incomprehension.

All afternoon Stephanie dreaded the seven-thirty evening rehearsal when the entire cast would see what a dreadful mistake they had made in their petition. She was bone-weary, as much from the emotional turmoil of the last twenty-four hours as from the lack of sleep. There had been no time to catch a wink all day.

When she entered the rehearsal room a cheer—"Yea, Stephanie"—went up, and the cast, applauding enthusiastically, beamed at her with hope in their eyes. Their optimism pierced her heart like a dagger. She knew what she would see in their faces before the evening was over.

Minutes before the rehearsal started, Nick, Phillip and Benedict, in turn, came to her with advice on Carmen's personality. Yes, yes, she knew—hot-blooded, gypsy. Earthy, sensual, uninhibited. She would try.

The rehearsal went just the way she knew it would. About ten o'clock, after they had repeated the "Habañera" scene at least seven times, Phillip asked, "Can we run that scene one more time, Stephanie?"

Close to tears, but determined not to break down, she merely nodded.

"I think we had better call it quits, Phil," Benedict said. "Stephanie's worn out. She didn't get any sleep last night, and she has worked all day straight through." Raising his voice, he called to the cast, "Thank you all for your hard work tonight. See you tomorrow."

Avoiding Stephanie's eyes, they all trooped out.

Her resources for stoicism running out, she fled through the back door and down to the beach. A thin crescent moon gave just enough light to touch the sea with an occasional quivery gleam. The tide was out, the surf quiet, and the dark, soft and enveloping. It was a relief to be safe from reproachful eyes and voices heavy with deliberate patience.

Within seconds she heard the pounding of footsteps behind her. Drat! It was Benedict, she knew. Hadn't he had enough of her today? Wearily she stopped and faced him.

"I know, Benedict. I need to make the character emotionally convincing. I've heard it at least a million times today, and your saying it again isn't going to do one bit of good. I don't want to talk about it. I don't want to talk about anything."

He rested his hands lightly on her shoulders. "That isn't what I was going to say. I was about to suggest that you sleep a little late in the morning, and we'll start at ten." He pulled her close and laid his cheek against her forehead. "I know you've had a rough day. I wish I could've made it better for you." Tenderly he kissed the place where his cheek had been. His tenderness brought her perilously close to the tears she had been holding back all day. When his lips touched hers softly with a kiss, she drew away abruptly.

"What's the matter?"

"Nothing. I just don't want to be kissed."

"That's a reasonable answer, I guess, but disappointing, to put it mildly."

"I suppose everything about me is disappointing to you right now."

Suddenly strong hands gripped her shoulders, and though she couldn't see in the darkness, she could feel the intensity of his eyes boring into her. "Look," he said, his voice almost angry in its earnestness, "let's get this straight. In spite of what happened today, I'm not disappointed in you. I don't understand it, and, of course, I wish things had gone differently. But I'm *not* disappointed in you."

Together they walked to Palmetto House, and Benedict went up with her to her door. After saying a brief goodnight to him, Stephanie collapsed on her bed, bone-tired and bleary-eyed, and propped her *Carmen* book up on her chest. If she memorized a certain number of pages each night, she would have it learned in time for the full dress rehearsals. She stared at the page, and the words and music all ran together. Desperate for sleep, she closed her burning eyes—for just two minutes, she promised herself. Then she'd really concentrate and get her work done. She sighed and wondered if she had behaved badly with Benedict.

Sometime later she awoke with a start to a still-lighted room, noted that it was two-thirty, turned off the light and went back to sleep without removing the book from her chest, undressing, or turning down the bedcovers.

The following days and nights all passed in a similar manner. From five o'clock each morning until late at night, it was study, study, study. She was not sure when Thursday turned to Friday—or even that it had. Never catching up on her sleep, she became more exhausted each day and drank increasingly more coffee to keep going. Her heart raced, she had trembling fits—the book in her hands actually shook during rehearsals—and her eyes felt as if they were lined with sandpaper. Her brain, she was sure, was all curled up and playing dead.

Through it all, night after night, Benedict's face hovered just above the printed page, his dark eyes intense with pity and hopelessness. She fancied that she saw the ravages of his despair etched permanently on his extraordinary face, and felt responsible. Her guilt drove her to more intense study and made her half sick with anxiety.

Benedict. She loved him so. She could hardly bear to think that in a few days they would part, with her love unspoken, arrested in the bud, never to blossom. And she would pursue her career, just as she had always planned. What was she to do about this love that so filled her, flooded her veins and throbbed with such exquisite agony?

Too soon came the night of the final dress rehearsal with everyone in full costume and makeup. It was their last chance to perfect their performance before opening night.

It was a fiasco. Everything that could go wrong, did. Silly things. Serious things. Stephanie was humiliated to the point of tears at forgetting words and missing entrances in the last act. It was a blessed relief to get to die just before the curtain fell at the end.

Stephanie knew that a great many of the things that went wrong could be remedied. The most serious of the problems—her unconvincing portrayal of Carmen and the low morale of the company leading to the lifeless and spiritless production—seemed irremediable. Though Benedict called for sharper rhythms and conducted with overlarge, vigorous gestures, and Phillip pled for more heart and soul, the consensus was that the opera was fated to be still-born. The gloom of defeat cast heavy shadows, and everyone's face wore the downcast look of lost causes. Stephanie bore the weight of it all on her weary shoulders and tried to keep a stiff upper lip.

The next morning, awake at five o'clock as usual, Stephanie studied her music until seven, then went down for an early breakfast. She was only halfway through her scrambled eggs when Benedict, rubbing his eyes and yawning, joined her.

"I couldn't sleep last night, Stephanie, for thinking about you. Do you think you could listen to some advice from a Dutch uncle?"

"I don't know. Dutch uncles grind you to pieces, don't they?"

"It's my intention to do it nicely," he said.

"Well, why don't you eat your eggs before they get cold? I'll wait," she answered, dreading another lecture about a sensual, earthy gypsy.

Talking around a mouthful of toast, he said, "What I'm going to say may sound stuffy, but I—oh, heck! I'm not going to apologize for how it sounds. I'm just going to say it."

"All right. I'm listening."

"What I was thinking last night is that music becomes a universal language only when it speaks of what it means to be human, and it does that by communicating emotions."

"I think I know all this, Benedict."

"Of course you do, but hang on a minute. The emotion in music, in opera, strikes a responsive chord in you, and you verify it by saying, 'Yes, that's true, because I've felt that way myself.' But if no emotion is there, then the music is merely a succession of sounds, pleasing perhaps, but dead as door nails." He set his coffee cup down and looked directly into her eyes. "It's the difference between the way a music box sounds and the way an orchestra sounds when it plays from its heart."

For Stephanie, his comparison was an inspired one. She thought immediately of her music box with its *Carmen*, a pretty little machine, dancing with mechanical precision to the predictable rhythms of the clockwork tune.

"Emotion, Stephanie—that's where the fire and sparkle, the soul and beauty come from. You know that, don't you? Well, the same thing is true for people. If we deny or suppress our emotions, we become dry and sterile, too; we lose part of our humanness. We lose touch with other people. Our backbones shrivel up and collapse. Perhaps not physically, but we become the living dead. Such a person can't bring music to life no matter if she has the most flawless technique in the world."

Stephanie noticed the change from "we" to "she" and felt a chill creeping along her spine.

"All of which brings me to the Dutch uncle bit. Now, sweetheart, I hope you'll take this in the spirit in which it's intended."

"I know. For my own good. I've probably heard it eighty thousand times the last three weeks, but go ahead."

"I have the feeling that you've been keeping the lid clamped so tightly on your emotions that you are just about to burst. Am I right?"

She stared at him without assent, then looked away, her heart pounding.

"I thought so." At the touch of his hand on her arm, she turned to face him again. Then he spoke very softly and slowly, with emphasis on every word. "It's no good this way. You're going to be tense and unhappy until you're able to give expression to the emotions you're bottling up. It may not be a life and death matter for you right now, but it is for your Carmen. You have within you everything it takes to make this Carmen come alive, to give her life and breath and sparkle. There is enormous power in emotions, if you will use it, if you will let go."

"I know, Benedict, but I can't. I'm afraid."

"Of what?"

"Of being exposed."

"As being human? Listen, sweetheart, people are not paying their good money to see you, Stephanie Morrison. They don't even know who you are. What they want is a Carmen who is—"

"I know—a hot-blooded, earthy, sensual, uninhibited gypsy."

"Let your emotions work for you, and don't be stingy with them, Stephanie. Open your heart wide and let them go free. This is the secret of it all." He caressed her arm and smiled deeply into her eyes. The conference was over, the Dutch uncle disappeared, and Stephanie and Benedict resumed eating their breakfast.

Counting the hours until curtain time, Stephanie hurried to the practice studio and settled down for some serious last-minute work. By nine o'clock, Benedict had found her again. "Are you all right? Can I help? Anything at all?" Then he hugged her, kissed her lightly on the lips and left, but not for long. Apparently he couldn't stay away. By lunchtime, she had received four hugs and kisses and some last-minute instructions. "Stephanie, after lunch I want you to go your room and get some rest. No more study. Do you hear? At five you may take a brief swim. At quarter to six I'm going to send up a tray with some soup and fruit on it. You'll insist you aren't hungry and can't eat, but I don't want you to try to sing on an empty stomach. You're going to need a lot of energy tonight. You do as I say, you hear?"

During the afternoon came a surprise wrapped in florist's paper. Inside was a single red rose and a card, which read, "Sing from your heart, my darling hot-blooded, earthy, sensual, uninhibited gypsy. That's all I ask. Love always from your hot-blooded, earthy, sensual, uninhibited gypsy admirer, Benedict." She laughed aloud. She couldn't remember the last time she had laughed; it seemed months ago. Back on her bed, she laid the rose across her heart and fell asleep.

She could have slept happily right on through swim time, but obediently did as she had been told and found the exercise relaxing, somewhat. Benedict was right about eating. She was far too nervous to be interested, but again followed his instructions to the letter. Just before leaving for the Music Center, she broke off the rose and tucked it into her bosom.

The moment she reached the backstage area, she felt the tension in the air. In make-up, the cigarette girls sat stiffly, eyes closed, speaking little. Every now and then a long-drawn breath was shakily exhaled, or a nervous, high-pitched laugh broke the brittle silence. In the dressing room, Stephanie stood with her head bent, avoiding eye contact with everyone as the costumer arranged the gathers in her blouse. The humiliation of failure had already settled upon her.

When she returned from her warm-up, Benedict, looking splendid in black tie, was waiting for her. "You are trembling all over." He kissed her and held her close. "Well, break a leg. I've got to run."

In a few minutes she heard applause and knew that he had taken his place at the podium in the orchestra pit. The overture began and Stephanie's heart broke into a race. The overture ended. The curtain opened to more applause. There was no turning back. The soldiers chatted, and Michaela came to look for Don José. Becoming increasingly jittery, Stephanie listened to those rambunctious little boys sing like angels for the changing of the guard. The cigarette girls sang of the pleasures of smoking. Stephanie's heart pounded in her throat. Next, the soldiers will ask, "But where is Carmencita?"

Clutching the rose in her bosom, Stephanie muttered, "Oh, God, I can't do this," and walked on stage.

Chapter Ten

Her knees threatened to collapse. Her heart hammered in her throat, and her mind went blank. Under the intense lights, she felt transparent. The music rushed past her like an out-of-control merry-go-round. Her eye measured the distance to the wing and the welcoming dark beyond.

In terror, she looked down into the semi-darkness of the orchestra pit. Benedict was staring straight at her, his face grim and tense, as he counted for her entrance. At his cue, she made her leap, and there was nothing to do but hang on and ride it out until the music stopped. She winced when she saw him immediately raise a hand to his lips to shush the orchestra. For tonight's *Carmen*, ladies and gentlemen, you will hear the cold, thin, colorless voice of a seventeen-year-old nun, who's holding on for dear life.

She looked at Nick and then at the other members of the cast in silent entreaty. "Help me. Help me." Their hollow eyes looked back helplessly from the ruins of their lost cause.

In desperation she sought Benedict again, and this time he smiled at her, beaming encouragement. In a little plea for passion, he laid his left hand over his heart. Her hand clutched the rose in her bosom. Then he smiled. It was one of their secret smiles that said, "You have the cutest ears," or "I'm working on a kiss for you, it'll be ready in about three hours."

It must have been the smile that triggered that sudden swelling of love in her heart. Her first impulse was to pull tight the reins until she regained control, but as the music whirled past her, she caught a glimpse of Benedict's eyes pleading with her. Go with love, they seemed to say. Give love its lead. Follow it and you won't go wrong.

I can't; I can't, she thought in panic, afraid of the uncharted territory ahead of her.

Benedict was watching her now with a strange intensity. The gypsy music called to her to follow. Timidly she let go of one of the reins. A sudden warmth flooded her body, and she yielded slightly to the hesitating, sharp-thrusting rhythms of the "Habañera." From the orchestra pit, Benedict's eyes burned. And deep in her heart, her love for him burned. The pain was exquisite; the very air around her seemed charged. I shall die, she thought. "Let go! Let go!" cried the music, spiraling around her.

She could hold back no longer. Closing her eyes, she dropped the other rein. With a tremendous surge of power, the primitive forces inside her broke through the little nun's chaste fears in an impassioned cry. And "L'amour," straight from the depths of Stephanie's heart, filled the hall.

She heard her voice return to her from the back wall—rich, warm, gloriously free, soaring above the sound of the orchestra.

In that moment a Carmen was born, already swiveling her hips and lifting her skirt to show an enticing flash of leg. Stephanie saw surprise leap in Don José's eyes and kindle into hope. From that one small spark, a flame flickered and grew. Stephanie, in wonder, watched the fire catch and spread from the cigarette girls to the young men, and heard it sizzle along the strings of the orchestra.

She felt herself being transformed, but as Carmen possessed her, she forgot the transformation. She became a bewitching child-woman, gypsy to the bone, filled with primal heat, who followed her passions wherever they might lead. Pagan that she was, she sang of love with uninhibited abandon and danced with a calculated seductiveness that made it very clear that she knew exactly where fire came from. When the wanton Carmen, with slow and sinewy motion, lifted her heavy hair from her neck, she, Stephanie, peered through the tangle of dark curls to steal a glance at Benedict. His dark horse, with a million dollars riding on its back, had just nosed ahead. Darling Benedict.

She flirted outrageously, made love to him with a hundred caresses and invitations in her voice, and then turned up the heat. He, in turn, followed her every lead, matched her and ended up showing her off like a jewel.

At the end of Act One, she took several curtain calls in a daze and then rushed headlong into the center of an explosion of ecstasy backstage. It was as if everyone's horse had won. Benedict came into the middle of it all, grabbed her and swung her around, laughing and whooping victoriously.

When the curtain fell on the final scene in which Carmen lay dead with the spurned José sprawled on top of her, there was a long silence followed by a tumultuous burst of applause. Then came the cry: a mighty roar of bravos. When Stephanie stepped in front of the curtain, the crowd went wild, and the bravos changed to bravas. She bowed deeply, and with tears streaming down her cheeks, accepted an armful of red roses. After several curtain calls, the audience began chanting "Encore."

In a hurried conference backstage, she and Benedict decided that she should sing the "Habañera" again. Just as she finished the aria, she drew the red rose from her bosom, kissed it and tossed it to Benedict. It missed him by a mile, but the audience loved it. Then after more applause and more bows, opening night was over.

After a late dinner at Valeriano's, Stephanie and Benedict strolled through the square. The streetlamps made patterns at their feet, and a little breeze stirred among the petunias, scattering their sweet fragrance. It was a night of a thousand voices. The fountain splashed, and in every tree, late summer insects clicked and whirred. From somewhere in the distance came a chorus of frogs horribly out of tune. Stephanie smiled. She'd bet Benedict could tune them up and make them musical. Was there any living creature that wouldn't sing for him?

She pressed closer to him, longing to bridge the waters of their undeclared love, to put an end to the agony of their separateness. To be lost in his kiss, in his arms, to merge into that state of oneness that she instinctively knew was the beginning and the end for all who loved.

He drew her close and held her tenderly for a few moments. The voices of the evening receded as Stephanie became aware of Benedict's quickened breathing. He touched his lips to hers, then showered her with dozens of brief, random kisses—on her ear, her hair, her throat, her cheek, her chin—leaving little hot spots that tingled pleasantly.

Then back to her waiting lips he came with an intense, demanding kiss. Stephanie moaned, lost in the throes of a primal passion. The tension was unbearable. She wanted release, but knew it would never come. Then she heard her own cry: great wracking sobs that she had no power to control.

She felt Benedict's surprise in his sharp release of her and in his stunned silence as he tried to gather his wits. Passion forgotten, he returned to her as a comforter. "Oh, Stephanie, my darling. It's all been too much for you, hasn't it?"

Or too little, she thought, unable to speak.

"I'd better get you home and to bed. This has been a big day for you. You must be exhausted."

Exhausted and disappointed. She wanted him to tell her he loved her. If he did, why didn't he say so?

The remaining five performances of *Carmen* were smash hits, more polished than opening night, if not quite so spontaneous. Every night the house was packed; the audience, enthusiastic. Stephanie's mother flew down from Virginia for one of the performances, and her friend, Cyndi McConnell, drove down from Charleston. Both of them met Benedict and loved him immediately. By the end of the run, Stephanie was beginning to feel like an old pro. Two newspapers sent reporters to interview her, and St. Cecelia's Rotary Club asked her to sing for one of their meetings. She loved every minute of it.

That last week in St. Cecelia passed in a golden blur of sunny days. It was as if she and Benedict had at last stumbled into a little corner of paradise where the garden never needed tending and time stood still, so they spent every possible moment together, intense and absorbed in each other.

They played hard. Stephanie wore herself to a frazzle trying to hit the tennis balls Benedict whacked over the net to her. She pedaled on weary legs all through one hazy afternoon, trying to keep up with him on a bicycle tour of the other end of the island. After their performances, they went for cooling midnight swims. When their tensions were all worked out, they would float on their backs, gently bobbing against each other. Benedict gazed into the heavens and named the stars for her.

Through it all, they talked endlessly. Stephanie marveled that they never ran out of things to say. During these times she studied him with a lover's absorption, fixing in her heart all the dear details of his face: the flash of his eyes, the smoothness of his cheeks, the sheen of his black eyebrows, the strength of his chin. She never tired of looking at him; she always discovered something new. Though a heartbreaking parting loomed ahead for them, they had agreed not to spend the entire week saying goodbye.

When the time came, they drove together in her Volkswagen to the Charleston airport. He was flying to Philadelphia to visit his parents before continuing on to New York. Their parting was bittersweet, filled with kisses that tore at her heart and promises to telephone and to write. They would not see each other again until December when she would be in New York to sing with Giuliano Sebastiani at the Lincoln Center. Before leaving Charleston, she stopped for a brief visit with Cyndi and then headed home for a few days with her mother.

Driving down the long, straight stretches of highway, Stephanie thought about Benedict. She wondered if he loved her as she did him, since he hadn't said a word about being in love. Was it possible that the relationship they had shared could have a different meaning for each of them? For her, it had been the stunning and intensely passionate experience of falling in love for the first time. Did he consider it as merely a summer romance to be enjoyed and then forgotten?

After all, he had said that even though he wanted a marriage and home someday, he was too busy with his career right now to think about it. It was not that she wanted to marry, either. Hadn't she made all those speeches about wanting one thing only—a career at the Met? She simply wanted her love to be reciprocated. It seemed to her that to love and to be loved would be quite satisfactory enough.

Stephanie's visit with her mother turned out to be a hectic one. There was so much to do and so many people to see. After one last morning of shopping and one final lunch, her mother drove her to the airport. Her arrival in Chicago, several hours later, marked the beginning of her career as Stephanie Morrison, opera singer.

All during those first days of September, she was terribly excited—meeting new people, finding her way around Chicago and most of all, learning new music. She threw herself into her work with all her old enthusiasm, determined to make every performance her best and to acquire the polish and poise she so admired in experienced singers. Benedict called at least twice a week, and she wrote him chatty little notes in spare moments.

After the newness of her situation began to wear off, images of Benedict intruded upon her work more and more. They broke her concentration and played havoc with her peace of mind. Missing him, she moped about, counting the hours until his next call, numbering the days until she would see him again. Her music suffered. Even though she was working with a director whom she admired and respected, she was convinced that her singing lacked the fire and sparkle it had had with Benedict. It was ironic, she thought, that she who had insisted all summer that she couldn't sing for Benedict, now discovered that she couldn't sing without him. How was she going to have a career at this rate?

October blew in, kicked up a swirl of orange and red leaves and skipped town, leaving the trees bare. November was tedious. It threatened to snow, changed its mind and threatened again. It strung out its days in such a slow progression that Stephanie, waiting in front of the calendar to mark off each day's end, thought she would scream. Would the next month never come?

Finally December fourteenth arrived in a flurry of snow. Stephanie was beside herself with excitement. Before this day was over, she would see Benedict. He was to meet her at the airport in New York.

The flight from Chicago to New York was uneventful. As her plane taxied to a halt in front of the terminal at Kennedy Airport, Stephanie could hardly remain seated long enough to hear the flight attendant wish the passengers a pleasant stay in New York City. Within moments after she entered the waiting area inside the building, she saw a hand shoot up above the heads of the crowd and wave. It was Benedict. His smile made her heart do somersaults. They started toward each other, zig-zagging through the press of waiting people. She couldn't get to him fast enough. Suddenly the way between them cleared, and she rushed into his outstretched arms with an ecstatic "Oh, Benedict!"

Breathless with happiness, they laughed aloud and then tightened their embrace with each new surge of joy, all the while taking care not to unsettle her black, wide-brimmed hat. Finally, he released her and stepped back. She watched him taking her in.

"You look nice. I like your coat. Just the color of crape myrtles."

"It's American Beauty red," she corrected primly, playing her part to the letter.

"You're going to have to take off that hat," he said, doing it for her. Her hair tumbled to her shoulders in a tangle of dark curls. He buried his face in it. "Oh, Stephanie, I've missed you so."

"I've missed you, too," she said.

While they were waiting for her bag, Benedict said, "Stephanie, you remember I told you I was going to talk to Jonathan Kraft about you. Well, I took him the tapes of your Introduction to the Opera and our *Carmen*, and he told me yesterday that he's very much interested. He wants you to sing for him sometime this afternoon. He thinks he may be able to work out something with the Met for you right away since your contract with Chicago is for one season only. Is that okay with you?"

"Okay? Oh, Benedict! I'm so happy I won't be able to sing a note. When do we go? Let's go right now before I get a stomachful of butterflies." She grabbed his arm and gave it an impulsive squeeze.

"After you've checked in at your hotel, we'll call from there and find out when he can see you," he suggested.

"You're such a good friend, Benedict."

"More than friend," he said smiling.

"Actually," he continued, "I'm not so altruistic as you think. I was motivated by purely selfish aims. I'm devising ways to get you to New York as soon as possible." He shot her a wicked grin.

After a hair-raising taxi ride into the city, they arrived at her hotel. The lobby, decorated for the holiday, was a wonderland of twinkling lights, garlands of greens and massed tiers of poinsettias. In the center, a giant Christmas tree reached for the ceiling. The festive atmosphere matched Stephanie's mood exactly. She just couldn't stop smiling.

In her room she waited patiently for the porter to set down her bag, turn on all the lights and open the curtains. The moment the door closed behind him, Stephanie said, "Let's call Mr. Kraft this very minute. I'm so excited I can't last much longer."

"First things first," said Benedict, holding out his arms to her.

She knew exactly what to do, and rushed into them. He picked her up and swung her around, and they ended the swing laughing ecstatically over the sheer joy of being together again. When he set her, reeling slightly, upon her feet, they exchanged dozens of kisses—on the nose, the cheek, the chin, the forehead, anywhere—all accompanied by innumerable little cries of surprise and delight. It was good to be in his arms again. She sighed happily.

"You don't know how I've longed for this," he said. "Three and a half months is a long time." After a moment he placed a soft, sweet kiss on her lips, paused to see how she liked it, and asked, "Would you like another?"

"Just a small one, please."

"I don't have any more small ones." Suddenly his lips were on hers with a passion that startled her at first. Then following his lead, she forgot everything around her and allowed herself to float away with him to the silent,

timeless world of their kiss, into which they poured all the
things lovers need to say to each other, but for which they
can never find the words. When their lips finally parted,
she clung to him weakly.

When she could speak again, she said in a small voice,
"Call up Mr. Kraft and tell him I've been kissed and can't
come."

"Nonsense. One more and you'll be perfectly restored," he said.

"Nonsense," she said. "One more and I won't even be
able to sing for Sebastiani tomorrow."

Reluctantly Benedict released her and made the telephone call. Jonathan Kraft told them to come over immediately.

After the audition was over, Benedict took her on a
tour of the Lincoln Center. On their way to see the hall
where she would be singing with Sebastiani, Benedict
said, "Jon was bowled over by you, I could tell. You were
absolutely splendid, as I knew you would be. I am so
proud of you."

Her hopes soared. They continued their tour and
sometime later came to the Opera House. As they stood
in the doorway and looked down at the stage, she could
hardly believe that the one great dream of her life was so
close to fulfillment. From where she stood, it was only a
short walk down the aisle to the stage. She laughed aloud
and looked up at Benedict.

"I can already see stars in your eyes," he said.

When they had finished the tour of the Center, in-
cluding the office where Benedict worked, he asked,
"Now that we have the rest of the afternoon free, what
in all of New York City would you most like to see? Af-

ter today, you're on your own. I have to work tomorrow.''

"Where you live," she said.

He laughed and said, "That's not exactly among the
top tourist attractions. You can see that anytime."

"Let's walk, then. I love to walk in new places, and
you can tell me about famous landmarks along the way.
I've always wanted to walk down Fifth Avenue. Could we
do that?''

By the time they returned to her hotel from their ex-
cursion, dusk had fallen. In every direction, Christmas
lights sparkled like jewels in the gathering darkness.

Having agreed during an early dinner to go to Benedict's apartment afterward, they left the restaurant in-
tending to catch a taxi. They discovered that it had started
to snow. Delighted, Stephanie tucked her hand into the
crook of Benedict's arm and insisted that they walk a few
blocks. How lovely it was to stroll by his side through the
snow, which swirled softly in the glow of the streetlamps
and settled as gently as goose down on the sidewalk!

"Oh, this is the most beautiful of nights," said Stephanie, gazing with pleasure at the wonderland-in-the-
making. "Don't you just love the snow, Benedict?"

"I like it more this minute than I ever have," he said,
smiling at her. "Shall we get our taxi, now?"

After a short ride, they arrived at his apartment. As he
opened the door, he said, "Well, here it is. There really
isn't much to see. It isn't very big." They took off their
coats and laid them across the back of a chair.

It was obviously a masculine environment, all beige
and blue colors. A grand piano, surrounded by stacks of
music, dominated the room. Behind the beige sofa that
invited you to curl up and listen to music, the wall was
covered with pictures of sailboats. On the bookshelves,

stuck in among the books, were several scale models of sailboats and even one inside a bottle.

"We never did go sailing," she accused him.

"We'll do it this summer, and that's a promise. Shall I make us some tea?"

"I'd love it, especially if you have Earl Grey."

When the tea was ready, he turned on his tape-player, and suddenly the room was filled with the sound of singing—a mezzo-soprano whose voice had a wonderful, warm golden quality. Stephanie looked at him sharply.

"That's me! That's the Introduction to the Opera music."

"Let's sit down and listen while we drink our tea," he said. They went to the sofa and cuddled up together. "I play that when I get to thinking about you. I've almost worn it out. That and the *Carmen*."

She looked at him but didn't say anything.

When the music stopped, she set her empty cup on the coffee table and turned to Benedict. "You know," she said, laying a hand on his arm, "I hope that you and I can work together again sometime. You'll be surprised to hear this, but recently I haven't sung nearly so well as I did for our *Carmen*. There is something about you that brings out the best in me." She looked at him earnestly.

"That's the nicest thing anyone has ever said to me. I'm surprised to hear you say it though, after what you've been through with me."

"Oh, what about what you went through with me? You were so patient. Anyone else would have given up. I learned so much from you, Benedict, but I didn't realize it until later."

"You had, by far, the harder part. You did an extraordinary piece of work. I was never so impressed by anyone as I was by you. You convinced me that there isn't anything you can't do. I wouldn't hesitate now to call on you for anything," said Benedict.

"Even the outrageous and the impossible? Like the *Carmen*?"

"Even the outrageous and the impossible," he repeated.

"Thank you," she said, touched and very pleased.

"I think we're a great team, Stephanie, now that we know how to work with each other. There's a lot of energy between us—a kind of electricity, a sort of magic, really."

After a few moments he went into the kitchen to get more tea. While he was gone, she went over to the piano where she saw three sheets of handwritten music. One of the pages was only half-completed, and the other two were marred by numerous changes and deletions. When he came back with the tea, she said, "I didn't know you were a composer, too."

"Not much of one, I'm afraid. I'm having trouble with it." He set the tea down on the coffee table, and she joined him on the sofa.

"What is it going to be?" she asked.

"It's supposed to be a trio for violin, viola and piano."

"Why isn't it going well?"

He looked at her for a long moment as if he didn't want to talk about it, then said, "Oh, I might as well tell you. I was thinking of it as a tribute to you, and in it I would express musically how I feel about you. But I'm discovering that I'm not any better at finding the notes than I am in finding the words. I make a lot of false starts, change my mind and try again."

He took a sip of tea, set it back on the table and turned to face her.

Here it comes, she thought, her heart throbbing in her throat. At last he was going to say the words she longed to hear. She gave him a soft, sympathetic smile that she hoped would encourage him.

He went for his tea again, drank half of it in desperate gulps before returning it to the table. He looked at her once more, his dark eyes blazing.

"I love you, Stephanie. I love you to distraction. I—I don't have the words to tell you properly how I feel about you. About all I can do is keep saying over and over that I love you."

"It was quite proper just the way you said it. I love you, too, Benedict. I love you so much." It was wonderful to be able to finally say it. Her heart was just about to burst with joy. He crushed her to him and held her close.

"But I hadn't intended to," she said.

"Hadn't intended to what?"

"Love you," she answered.

"I know. Your career. What happened?"

Cradled in his arms she said, "I guess love didn't know it was against the rules to steal into the heart of a career woman."

"When did it happen, Stephanie?"

"I don't know. I didn't realize it until the night Dierdre's shoe hit you. You were lying on your bed with one sock on wrong side out. When I saw your sock, I knew. I don't know why, but it was so crazy and unromantic, I laughed."

"I remember," he said.

"Were you in love with me then?" she asked.

"Yes, very."

"When did you first know?"

"I was coming down with it that Sunday you went to Charleston. I suspected that my reason for going after you in such a cockeyed way was more than just to get things straightened out. I was afraid of losing you. I had a full-blown case—all the classic, text-book symptoms—by that night we made our truce, and it's been getting worse ever since."

"It's not a disease, Benedict."

"When I'm not with you, it's worse than a disease."

"You've known it a long time, then. All summer and you didn't say a word," she said, moving out of his embrace and turning to look at him with sweetly accusing eyes.

"You weren't ready to hear it. You fought it like a tigress. You weren't going to have any part of it, and you made that quite clear. Remember all those speeches about how you were going to be a career woman with no love and no marriage and no compromise?"

"A woman can change her mind," she said.

"Stephanie, I'm going to ask you to do something outrageous and impossible."

She almost stopped breathing.

"Will you marry me, Stephanie?"

She smiled and nodded her head, for, suddenly, she couldn't speak. He kissed her then and gathered her into his arms tenderly as if she were too fragile and precious to risk to the rigors of the impossible and the outrageous. She snuggled happily against him.

"I'm not afraid anymore," she said.

"Good," he murmured against her hair. "Of what?"

"Of compromises. Of marriage and a career."

"Marriage? Oh, good heavens!" Suddenly, he released her and sat bolt upright. "How could I have forgotten?"

A chilling alarm ran through her. She could hardly choke out the question. "What is it, Benedict?"

"We just became engaged, didn't we?" He looked flustered and embarrassed, the first time she had ever seen him so.

"I thought so, maybe not." She wanted to cry.

He reached into his pocket and drew out a small box. He looked at her apologetically and said, "I've been thinking of this moment for months, and now when the time comes, I lose my head. I wish I was better at this sort of thing, Stephanie."

"You're doing fine, really. Just keep going," she said, smiling at him, finding his discomposure strangely endearing. She loved him so. He continued to sit looking at her, holding the little ring box, unopened.

In a moment he took out the ring, kissed it and slipped it on her finger. "I love you, my beautiful gypsy."

"I love you, too, so much," she said, and then held out her newly adorned hand so they both could admire the ring. "Look how it sparkles!" she said, turning it this way and that in the light. "It's so beautiful."

They sat smiling at each other for a moment or two and then exchanged tender kisses.

"Should we talk about a wedding day, do you think?" she asked. "Our families are going to ask us that the first thing."

"You're right. I'm lucky to be marrying an older woman to help me do this thing properly," he said.

"Older?" she repeated, puzzled.

"Yes, you told me you were thirty."

"That was last summer," she said. "I'm twenty-three now."

"You changed. Good for you. I know several women who keep the same age for several summers."

"Benedict! Be serious. We need to decide on a date before we call our families."

"What do you think about June the twelfth?" he asked.

"That's Black Friday."

"Oh, no. That's the day we met. It was a very good day."

"June the twelfth it shall be, then. Let's invite Lynne and Nick."

"Let's ask them to sing," Benedict suggested.

"I am the happiest, luckiest woman in the world."

"And I am the happiest, luckiest man."

His dark eyes were shining as he put his arms around her and pulled her close to him again. Their lips met and the world dropped away. They were lost in each other's embrace, in the ineffable sweetness of their kiss. It was both gentle and strong. It demanded nothing but their pledge of love and promised them everything.

*   *   *   *   *

Silhouette Romance®

LONG, TALL TEXANS

AWARD OF EXCELLENCE

Diana Palmer brings you the second Award of Excellence title

SUTTON'S WAY

In Diana Palmer's bestselling Long, Tall Texans trilogy, you had a mesmerizing glimpse of Quinn Sutton—a mean, lean Wyoming wildcat of a man, with a disposition to match.

Now, in September, Quinn's back with a story of his own. Set in the Wyoming wilderness, he learns a few things about women from snowbound beauty Amanda Callaway—and a lot more about love.

He's a Texan at heart ... who soon has a Wyoming wedding in mind!

The Award of Excellence is given to one specially selected title per month. Spend September discovering *Sutton's Way* #670 ... only in Silhouette Romance.

RS670-1R

You'll flip . . . your pages won't!
Read paperbacks *hands-free* with

Book Mate • I

The perfect "mate" for all your romance paperbacks

**Traveling • Vacationing • At Work • In Bed • Studying
• Cooking • Eating**

Perfect size for all standard paperbacks, this wonderful invention makes reading a pure pleasure! Ingenious design holds paperback books OPEN and FLAT so even wind can't ruffle pages — leaves your hands free to do other things. Reinforced, wipe-clean vinyl-covered holder flexes to let you turn pages without undoing the strap . . . supports paperbacks so well, they have the strength of hardcovers!

Pages turn WITHOUT opening the strap.

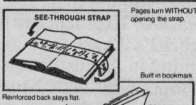

SEE-THROUGH STRAP

Reinforced back stays flat.

Built in bookmark

BOOK MARK

BACK COVER HOLDING STRIP

10" x 7¼ opened.
Snaps closed for easy carrying, too

Available now. Send your name, address, and zip code, along with a check or money order for just $5.95 + 75¢ for postage & handling (for a total of $6.70) payable to Reader Service to:

> Reader Service
> Bookmate Offer
> 901 Fuhrmann Blvd.
> P.O. Box 1396
> Buffalo, N.Y. 14269-1396

Offer not available in Canada
*New York and Iowa residents add appropriate sales tax.

BM-G